"Ha! ha! mine! mine!" cried the pretended Abbot, as seizing Emeline in his arms he dashed off, at full speed toward the forest.

THE ILLUSTRATED

# GARDEN OF ROMANCE,

CONTAINING THE FOLLOWING

## TALES AND ROMANCES:

———————

FANNY GREENWELL, OR THE OLD FARM HOUSE.

EMELINE, OR THE LOVE PLEDGE.

THE RIVAL KINGS, OR THE MAGIC FISH.

THE ABBESS,

ETC.

———————

LONDON:

PRINTED AND PUBLISHED BY W. HALL,

18, UPPER CLEVELAND STREET, NEW ROAD.

1843.

# PENNY ILLUSTRATED

# GARDEN OF ROMANCE

**ADDRESS:** KIND AND COURTEOUS READER,—We have this day the pleasure of introducing to your notice No. 1, of "THE PENNY GARDEN OF ROMANCE." Well we know, "'tis not in mortals to command success," but we will do more---endeavour to deserve it. And this, we think, may be looked upon as a fair specimen of the style in which the work will in future be produced; but we, nevertheless, assure our readers, that a liberal patronage upon their part, will operate as a stimulant to increased exertions on ours. Fearlessly, therefore, we launch our little barque on the tide of public opinion, trusting it may be steered into the safe harbour of general approbation. To our respected brethren in the trade we can only say, we start in opposition to none; hence (in the words of a celebrated lord, when putting forth a fly from his window) may they one and all generously exclaim, "Go, little wanderer, there is room enough in the world for me and for thee." Having said for ourselves thus much, we respectfully don our editorial *chapeau*, and retire; though we cannot do so without breathing a wish that, that sweet sunshine to the heart--woman's smile, may cheer us in our agreeable pursuit, and give to our exertions the countenance of that support which never fails to ensure success.

# FANNY GREENWELL;

## OR,

# THE OLD FARM HOUSE.

### CHAP. I.

> Arouse ye, from your sleep awake,
> Morning opes her golden eye,
> Rosy beams in beauty break
> Over ocean, earth, and sky.

WELL, George was right; he said the thunder-storm last night would bring a lovely morning, and what can be more beautiful? the air is fresh and pure, and the earth is brightened by the rising sun. This is a happy home; all are content, and labor seems delight.

No. 1.

Such were the words uttered by Sophia Greenwell, the elder of two daughters, whose sire (James Greenwell) occupied a neat farm house, distant about thirty miles from London.

She was standing in the farm-yard, gazing intently on the bright sky, which presented a strange contrast to its appearance on the preceding night, when the earth had been visited by a terrific thunder-storm. The east was now decked with the brightest tints of crimson and sparkling gold; the beauteous flowrets of lawn and forest once more raised their glowing petals to meet the rays of the sun; myriads of birds flitted from spray to spray, scattering the glittering dew-drops, and filled the balmy air with their melodious warblings.

After enjoying the many beauties around her for a short time, a love-sick village swain, named Mat Maythorn, entered the farm yard.

"Hey-day, Mathew! what ails you?" said Sophy, observing his dejected appearance.

"I don't know, Miss Sophy," said he, "I be a strange lad."

"Indeed!" said Sophy, smiling.

"Yes, I bean't like another mortal being; I think I'm an evil spirit as they calls it; I'm not myself, abroad or at home, at work or at play, awake or asleep—nothing pleases me, I'm always a grumbling."

"And yet," said Sophy, "you used to be so cheerful, so willing, and so obliging."

"Ah! I didn't know trouble then," said Mat, sighing. "You'd hardly believe it, when Aunt Madge died, and they told me of it, I was hard at work, I blubbers a bit, and then I sets too a whistling, and they called me a pig, but I didn't mind 'em, for Aunt Madge left me in her will a matter of seven pound ten, so I thought I was a made man, but I warn't."

"Why you were rich, Mathew!"

"Oh yes, I wur independent enough for a while," rejoined Mat, "but I warn't long afore I wur as poor as a church mouse!"

"How came that to pass?" asked Sophy.

"Ah! she has a power to answer for," sighed, Mat abstractedly.

"Whom?" again interrogated Sophy.

"Betty Wibbles," answered Mat. "You'd hardly believe me, Miss Sophy, that lass turned me topsy-turvy, she ruinated me quite!"

"You don't say so?" said Sophy, with a laugh.

"Yes, I do; I took to playing at all fours, and 'dulging in other luxuries!"

"Indeed, Mat!"

"Yes, drat me! I wouldn't be content with fourpenny, but I must swill sixpenny ale; I wore my Sunday clothes while money lasted, and I wore 'em out, I was mortal extravagant—was a regular dash, chaps won my money, and Becky laughed at me; so I opens my eyes, and I says to myself, Mat, says I, whoah, it's time to stop, and sure enough it wur, for Madge's seven pound wur all gone, and I'd nothing left but seven shillings, so I turns to work again, and all goes on pretty fairly till—"

"Till what?" interrupted Sophy.

"Bob Bags the post boy comes up to Becky Wibbles and claps a letter into her hands," continued Mat. "Lard, if you'd only ha' seen she ump for joy! I thought the wench wur going to strikes! I couldn't make it out no how soever, when she says to I, Matty, says she, look at that there!"

"And what was it?" asked Sophy.

"She ca'ed it a *Wollytine*—it wur a queer looking affair. I'll be shot if there warn't a heart a' most as big as a bullock's, with two thingumbobs stuck through it just so," said Mat, crossing his fingers by way of illustration; "there wur a lot o' varses too," continued Mat; "she said they wur beautiful, and cum'd all the way fra' Lunnun from Jemmy Jenkins, and then she falls too a giggling again. Ah! says I, I only wish Mr. Jemmy Jenkins wur here, I'd larrup he well wi' cart whip—I'd gi' him a lesson for his *Wollytines*!"

"Ha, ha, ha!" cried Sophy.

"She be tittering at me, too," muttered Mat inwardly. "They calls women the soft sex, but I'll be shot if they arn't as hard as a horse-shoe. Miss Sophy," cried he at length. "I want to ax thee a question, if thee'lt be good enough to answer it."

"What is it, Mat?"

"Don't you think me a very passable chap?" said he, standing as erect as possible.

"Very so!" returned Sophy.

"Then that for Madam Becky," cried the rustic, snapping his fingers, she arn't no judge howsomdever! I knowed as much myself, I can see it —bless you, when I looks in the polished pewter—we dont want a looking glass at home. Only thou wait till thou see'st me in my spic span new frock, and highlows without hobnails, and then you'll say some'at indeed. I'll make up my mind, I'll treat Becky wi' difference, drat me if I don't; oh, oh, lard, here be measter coming," he continued, glancing somewhat anxiously toward the cottage. "Do'ee be good natured, Miss Sophy— doant'ee say you seed me, and I'll take all thy letters to George Rutly, and say nothing to nobody."

"Away with thee, then," said Sophy; "quick!"

Mat needing no second bidding—rushed hastily from the spot.

---

## CHAP. II

"If I could waft away this low-hung mist,
If I could unbind this burning brand
That lightens round my heart."—

MATURIN.

A FATHER'S LOVE—THE PARADISE OF SWEETS—A SQUIRES' VISIT TO SOME
PERSONS PROVE A BANE.

The Farmer now came forth from his dwelling, bearing in his hand a letter which he had received from George Rutly, soliciting the hand of his daughter Sophia in marriage. They had been playmates almost from childhood, till at length, as their ages increased, love, pure as the breath of angels, usurped the place of friendship, and now

—————————"They were never
Weary, unless when separate;'

"Yes, George," soliloquised Greenwell, who was still gazing upon the letter; it is the act of an honest man, thou hast taken a step that reflects on thee credit. I cannot deny thee thy wish, though the granting it bring sorrow and regret, for I shall miss my careful housewife sorely. It seems to me but a year or two, since she was a merry light-hearted girl, nimble as a fawn.

"Her voice was the warble of a bird,
So soft, so sweet, so delicately clear,
That finer, simpler music ne'er was heard."

My blooming girl! my tender helpmate! when thou art gone I shall indeed feel thy mother's loss more keenly!"

"Father! dear father!" cried Sophy rushing up to his side.

"Ah! Soph, girl, ever on the watch, ever busy about the farm," said Greenwell, "thou'rt a good girl, a right good girl! Kiss me! Bless thee lass, I ought to be, and I *am* proud of thee! Where's Fanny?"

"In her paradise of sweets as she terms it," answered Sophy. "Ever since Squire Melville sent old Prune with the exotics from the Manor Grounds, early and late, her very heart seems set upon them. But why do you look so sorrowful my Father?"

"I'll tell thee Sophy, for thou art prudent, I like not these gifts, this tinted produce of the earth; these beauteous flowers, though they may adorn her little garden, may be the innocent means to corrupt a heart pure as the buds themselves. Fanny is young and childish, too prone to flattery, loves not her plain, her happy home, prizes not the smiles of her sister, or her father."

"I must not hear you say so, dear father," said Fanny; "in thought you wrong her. She is all heart, for I have witnessed when you chid and left her presence, she would cry bitterly, and often has she said to me, 'sister, you are a happy girl, our father loves you, never scolds nor is angry with you—tell me your secret, I will strive to learn it.'"

"Did she? did she?" faltered Greenwell, much affected. "It is a father's fond affection feeds this harshness—it is the outpouring of a heart perhaps too sensitive to fear. Since thy mother died the world has thriven with me; but what is worldly wealth my girl, weighed against the riches of the heart; I'd rather be a beggar wending my weary way through the world with my poor and innocent children around me, than the richest man that ever stepped; and they were severed from their home, the home to which they are ever welcome—their father's heart."

"Fear not for Fanny, father, I would stake my life upon her duty."

"And so would I," said Greenwell, "but I have seen and proved mankind—have awoke to sense of injury—have known deceit—allurement, (and there are many snares for the unwary; the young mind needs the maturer hand of age to guide it safely through this busy world. Fanny is artless, and a cunning flatterer might easily mislead her."

*( To be continued.)*

EMELINE

# EMELINE;
### OR,
## THE LOVE PLEDGE,
### AN OLD ENGLISH ROMANCE.

#### BY JOHN HEATHER,
*Author of " Emma Darnley," &c. &c.*

___

## CHAP. I.

—— " The hour's now come ;
The very minute bids thee ope thine ear ;
Obey, and be attentive."
          SHAKSPEARE.

### A MORNING RAMBLE—ITS RESULTS.

THE heavens displayed a lovely morning, and myriads of brilliants suspended from every leaf, when Sir Calthart Burgoyne, accompanied by a fine mastif dog, sallied forth from his villa, and struck into a daisy-clad path leading through the forest of Shadwell. Sir Calthart, unlike many of his age, which did not yet exceed twenty-five, delighted to wander over the sunny hills to see the meadow flowers bloom and fade in spring, the hedges and streams put on their luxuriant array of graceful weeds at midsummer, and to watch for the lovely hoar frost enrobing the leafless trees in silver and gems in winter; and at the time of which we write, he wandered silently on by the side of a crystalline stream, that murmured over a pebbly bed, fringed with wild blossoms. At last, however, his progress was intercepted by an elevation of the ground, thickly studded with dwarf trees. At this juncture the dog gave sudden utterance to a low growl, and a sound of voices fell on the knight's ear. Resolving to ascertain from whence the sound came, Calthart advanced, and, threading his way as silently as possible through the closely intertwined underwood, at length succeeded in getting a good view of the speakers in question, who were standing in a glen considerably beneath him, engaged in deep converse. The one was a tall dark personage, whose piercing eyes were as black as the raven's plume. He was habited in a long sable cloak, and round felt hat, ornamented with a tall black feather. The other's dress was something similar, with the omission of the head ornament.

The young knight, motioning his dog to silence, now listened with eager attention to the following dialogue, carried on between them in the most earnest manner—

"She—she must be mine—she shall be mine!" exclaimed one of them passionately.

"And yet thou rejectest the means by which thou canst obtain her," rejoined the other. "Why not let me rid thee of this rival? Emeline can then—"

"No, Freeman, no!" interrupted the other hastily, "I—I cannot resort to such an act to gain her;—to—to murder him—him, who—oh, horror, horror!" and the speaker buried his face in his hands. "No," resumed he, after a pause, "the youth, Calthart Burgoyne, *shall* not be injured; if blood is to stain the earth, let it be mine—if life must be sacrificed, I—I will be the victim!"

"It's strange this young blade should possess such influence over thy feelings," said Freeman.

"It—it may be," returned the other; "but thou hast heard my commands, and mark me, have a care that no harm befal him."

"From me he has nought to fear," said Freeman; "but, ignorant of thy pleasure, I yesterday ordered his death, and should he fall in the path of any one of the band, his doom is inevitably sealed."

"Great God!" vociferated the other, "a—a—nother murder to my charge—mother and son both hurried from existence by my villany! Oh! Uberto, 'twere better to have perished 'neath the banners of thy country, than thus lived to become a cold-blooded and heartless assassin!"

A fearful pause followed this outburst, during which time it was evident the speaker was enduring extreme mental agony. At length, as though his senses were bewildered, he bitterly exclaimed—

"See, see! there is his mother's shade! Ah! it bids me approach. I—I come—I come!" and throwing his mantle from him, the unhappy man rushed toward the object of his vision.

He had not proceeded far, however, ere he fell swooning to the earth. Seeing what had occurred, his companion hastily advanced, raised him from the earth's green garmenture, and drawing from his vest a singular looking flask, applied it to his companion's lips. The pungency of its contents was apparent by the almost instantaneous restoration of the swooning man's senses.

"Why this dreadful emotion?" cried Freeman, as the other gazed listlessly about him; "what crime hast thou committed, that its bare recollection can thus unman thee?"

"What crime!" echoed the other, with fearful emphasis. "What crime is that which haunts the soul of man with fearful visions—visions that are ever gliding before him like a perpetual tormentor, at home, abroad, by night, by day, still, still the same; but no more of this, away with thee, Freeman, I will meet thee at the owlet's haunt two hours hence—away!"

"Aye! at the owlet's haunt?" laughed the other, as he disappeared among the bushes; "by St. Alfred! that's a brilliant appellative for the old castle ruins and its nest of night birds. Ha, ha!"

The bandit chief (for such *he* was who now remained) again seemed calling to mind some bad act of his past life; ever and anon would he sigh and gaze wildly around him, his dark eye swelling with emotion. At length, in a tone of the deepest emotion, he exclaimed—

"Oh! Eleanor, my—my once loved Eleanor! what demon possessed me when I drew my treacherous blade and plunged it into thy fair bosom? when—when shall I be freed from the appalling sound of—of thy death shriek, preceded, too, by those ominous words, 'we shall meet again, Uberto!' oh! horror, horror!" and the man of blood, licking his parched lips, looked as timidly about him as though he actually expected to confront the object of his soliloquy. "Hist! what hear I?" he continued at length, "ah! 'tis a troop of horse, coming this way too, I must away." So saying, the robber, springing into an adjacent thicket, instantly disappeared.

The fact of a troop of horse approaching was but a mere phantasy, though certain it was some such sounds were borne on the balmy air. The disappearance of Uberto was, however, an easement to our young friend in the thicket, who, rising from his rather uneasy position, hastened homeward, and throwing himself on a couch pondered deeply upon the strange events of his ramble, and what he had so singularly heard.

---

## CHAP. II.

——— "Answer me, spirit, say
Who art thou? what's thine errand here? and why
Thou dost appear before me in that shape
Of awful mystery?"
CONSCIENCE.

THE MYSTIC WARNING—THE PLAN—AND THE DISGUISE.

AFTER the chieftain's hasty exit from the forest glen, and from whence he had—though unknown to himself—been watched by Calthart Burgoyne, he bent his steps slowly towards the place he had appointed to meet the band. As he approached the place of rendezvous, he came in sight of a meandering stream, that from its beauty attracted his notice. Though he had seen it oft before, 'till now it never seemed to possess so charming an appearance, and the little wavelets, caused by a slight breeze which fanned the face of nature, appeared like so many glittering brilliants sparkling in the sunbeams, with a lustre almost indescribable.

Uberto ascended a high hill, the top of which was covered with fern. When he attained the summit, a most sublime prospect opened itself to his view, and the surrounding objects presented themselves in striking magnificence. At a distance a village, enveloped as it were in a dark wood ; a little in advance grew a thick labyrynth of bushes ; near the hill side (which at this distance appeared beneath the sunbeams like a sheet of molten gold) run the stream, spreading itself in various fantastic windings ; at the margin grew a luxuriant profusion of that innocent little flower, 'the true lover's emblem,' need we say the ' forget-me-not ?' Amid these, quantities of king-cups raised their golden crests, standing out as it were in bold relief against the former, whilst above him was the bright blue sky, richly decked with clouds of surpassing beauty.

The robber, who had been gazing with rapture upon the scene, now felt a drowsy sensation creep over him. Spreading, therefore, his huge cloak upon the green sward, he laid himself down to rest.

It wanted still an hour to the time he had appointed to meet his band ; indulging, therefore, the dictates of nature, he soon fell asleep. How long his slumbers would have continued 'tis not for us to suppose, but, ere he had slept many minutes, he was roused from them by music the most delightful, something resembling that of an harp, accompanied by a clear soft voice, which sang, or rather chaunted, the following—

### MYSTIC WARNING,

' Uberto, Uberto ! beware, beware !
How you fall in the wily serpent's snare ;
Thy deeds to the world are clear and plain,
They ne'er by thee can be hid again.
Exposed is the haunt of thy valiant men,
Thro' thy meeting this morn in the forest glen !
Listen ! to this prophetic lore,
' Uberto, Uberto ! thy reign's nigh o'er.'

' List to the song that your harper sings,
Beware of the danger that folly brings ;
Strange tho' the music seems to be,
It comes a warning voice to thee.
Take then thy choice of weal or woe,
Of danger that none but you can know ;
Here's Heaven's decree, I dare say no more,
Uberto, Uberto ! thy reign's nigh o'er !'

' Again, before I bid adieu !
From the world of spirits I came to you,
To warn thee of danger that soon shall be
Close on thy wake like a stormy sea.
Thy name—thy hands are stain'd with blood,
Thy deeds are stamp'd, with the curse of God ;
This night—' but I must say no more,'
Uberto, Uberto ! thy reign's nigh o'er !'

(*To be continued.*)

# GARDEN OF ROMANCE.

## FANNY GREENWELL;
### OR,
### THE OLD FARM HOUSE.

[*Continued from our last.*]

At this moment, the object of their solicitude came tripping lightly towards them.

"See Sophy, see!" said Fanny, holding forth a pretty bunch of flowers; "they match the rainbow's brightness—are they not beautiful? I've cut them from the stem before their sweetness faded—I've brought them for father."

"For me!" sighed the farmer, taking the nosegay; "artless child, I'll wear them for my Fanny's sake. Their colors are bright and varied; these glittering hues would soon perish before the warm sun, but here is one that would not die so speedily, it is a briar—a thorn; what made you pluck it?"

"To prop their tender stems," said Fanny.

"Fit emblem of the world's way," rejoined Greenwell; "these flowers are like a young girl's life—in her early home she blooms fresh and beautiful; the days pass on and the gazer views with delight the charming flower; then comes a longing round the heart to possess it; 'tis plucked, worn awhile, and prized there—shortly it droops and needs a prop, (of thorns she finds abundance,) at length it withers and its bloom dies. Had it remained in its humble soil, it had not died so soon."

"I do not understand you father," said Fanny timidly.

"Then I will be plain with thee Fanny, 'tis fit I should be so—the young squire is not we'come here to me, his motives are not prompted by honor, his presents and flowers are but lures to win a flower to me more precious—that flower is thee, Fanny."

"I understand you now, clearly understand you. Father you shall have

No. 2.

no cause to prompt these fears—no flower, the squire's gift shall live."
She would have rushed from the spot, but was detained by Sophy. " Do
not stay me Sophy;" said she, "no act or deed of mine *can* please my
father, this one perhaps may."

" 'Tis a headstrong girl, to whom unwelcome sounds the council of a
parent," said Greenwell—" what would avail the destruction of those plants
if the giver found a welcome here?   I forbid your meetings: you may
deem me harsh, Frances, I speak for your welfare; you do not yet know
how terribly harsh a father can be when urged by act of disobedience—
but we'll drop that theme, nay, more, we will not speak of it again; you
are not unmindful of your duty, and I feel assured will ne'er betray it—
there, I'm not angry—George Rutly will be here to-day,—'twill not be
long ere will come a happy day to one, though not perhaps to me."

' What day, father?"

" Thy sister's bridal day," replied Greenwell; " he asks my consent to wed
her.    He is worthy, honest, and beloved, (the blood mounts in thy face,
Soph, and that's a tell-tale); I have no plea to refuse him save one—"

" And that :—

" Is a selfish lurking round my heart that tells me I can ill spare my
girl," faltered Greenwell, placing his hands upon her shoulders, and gazing
at her affectionately.

" Happy Sophy, said Fanny, soliloquising, Thou hast all a father's love,
thou art fortune's favorite child; but although I sorrow, I will not envy
thee."

" Thou wilt soon have another heart to cheer with thy smile of good-
nature," said Greenwell to Sophy; " who shall then give such welcome to
your father?"

" My sister Fanny," rejoined Sophy; she, I am sure, will strive to make
you happy."

" She will," said the farmer, taking Fanny smilingly by the hand;—
" hold up thy eyes, girl; ere thy sister leaves us she must teach thee the
housewife's duty; thy heart is warm and willing, and a dullard will not
be her pupil."

" Ah! father, I would strive night and day to see you happy—to win
your smile, and such a smile as beamed but now upon me.   The Squire
shall come no more—I will forget I ever knew him—unheeded shall be
the flowers that bring him, when absent, to my memory; my home shall
be my father's hearth—my only thought his happiness."

" Bless you," said Greenwell, kissing her affectionately; " but come,
girls, come to your household duty—look to the maids within, I'll see to
the men without; see the sun has risen high, and, unless I'm by, there
will be idlers in the five-acre field! What with Sophy's wedding and the
sports of the harvest-home, our farm will shortly be the abode of jollity!
Good morning, girls, good morning!"

" Kind, generous father," said Sophy, as the farmer left them; " it will
grieve me much to be separated from thee.—Fanny will win his heart—
he will have no other to share it."

" I'd hate thee if I deemed you thought so!" cried Fanny; " that is
the first ungenerous reflection I ever heard you break towards me, and it
grieves me! Often, how very often had I cause to think so, and still I
murmured not—I shed tears, but no eye saw them; I was a lone, heed-

less thing; his voice seldom welcomed, or his smile cheered me—they were all thine. And yet I envied thee not! You were ever his confidant, his adviser—what was I? a worthless being, to whom a kindness were a condescension. Do not weep, dear Soph, our father will love you ever; the little I shall steal will not beggar you much. Your heart will waken to another and a new love—the love of a husband, Soph, perhaps to innocents, who soon will *strip* my father of his share!"

"Oh, never! Fanny, if Heaven wills it so, I should love them dearly, but nature would be dead when I forgot my father, he who has been throughout my life so good, so very good!"

"Come, we'll talk no more of that," said Fanny; "and thou art to become a bride—how sweet the title—there thou art again chosen by fortune. No George Rutly comes to me to stroll on summer nights or chat before the winter's fire—no George Rutly comes on Sabbath mornings to beau me to the village church—no George Rutly whispers fond things in my ear—no George Rutly, at the casement in the moonlight, steals the loving kiss."

"Fanny!"

"It's true—I've seen and heard it oftentimes and something whispered to my heart, that Sophy was created to be loved."

"And so art thou, dear Fanny; there liveth none so humble on the earth but owns some love. But you mistake—you own a father's, a sister's fondest, firmest love; and for a beau, I know of one who'd fain find favor in your eyes."

"Cold, cold must be his love, whose heart owned not the courage to reveal it!" said Fanny. "Tell me who it is?"

"Michael Wright," replied Sophy.

"Michael Wright! You're jesting, surely?"

"Believe me, no!"

"What, Michael Wright! the modest Michael Wright! he who stammers in his speech and never looks you in the face? why, if you chance to meet him of a morning and bid him good morrow, "Aye, aye, miss," he replies; "foine for young wheat!"—then should the sky look lowering, and you tell him it is dull, its—"Yeaz, yeaz, bad, bad for the hay; but charming for the tares!" No, no, Michael Wright must seek another love—he's no fit swain for Fanny Greenwell."

"Why? he's a farmer's son, our equal, Fanny—an honest, industrious young man, with a good heart, and he will, I'm sure, make you happy."

"That he never will!" said Fanny.

"Be not so hasty in your conclusion; he will, I'm sure he will; though you may not like him now, he'll be your husband, and I shall live to see it;"

Their converse was now interrupted by the abrupt appearance of Mat Maythorn, who seemed much agitated.

"What's the matter, Mat?" asked Sophy.

"Mischief's the matter—Beckey Wibbles is the matter"—replied Mat; "there she is, as impudent as a turkey-cock, sitting a top o' the stile waiting for Bob Bags, the post boy, with the answer to the *wollytine* in her hand. If I was to knock Bob Bags down and take the letter, would that be robbing the mail? if it aint, I'm blowed if I don't!"

"You'll be hanged if you *do*!" said Sophy.

"Oh, Beckey Wibbles! Betty Wibbles! you see how near she's brought me to an untimely end! oh, that precious wollytine!"

"Valentine you mean, Matthew," said Fanny.

"Well, I said wollintine!" rejoined Mat; "if I didn't, you blame Becky Wibbles and not me—what do they mean by a wollintine?"

"'Tis a day of the year (the 14th of Febuary)" returned Fanny, "when they say the first unmarried person you meet you are destined to wed—it is a day on which lovers send their tokens."

"What, anything in the shape of a large heart, stuck through cris-me-cross?"

"Yes," replied Fanny, "that's a lover's heart pierced by Cupid's darts —but why do you ask me? I know nothing of valentines, cupids, and darts!"

"Don't you? Heigho! I wish I did'nt," sighed Mat. "I smell a rat—Wollytines day, the 14th of Febuary—that is six months ago. Phew! I'm a cake; it aint no wollytine at all! she's trying to make me jealous. Ha, ha, ha! But she won't though—I'm so thankful Miss Fanny you've made me so happy. Oddzooks!" cried he, "I was almost forgetting— that's no wonder for I am almost beside myself for joy—Miss Fanny, mum! there's somebody waiting for you near the copse."

"Whom?" asked Fanny.

"Young Squire; he bid me tell 'ee—"

"Fanny!" said Sophy.

"I need no second remembrance, dear Sophy.—Mathew, you say I've made you happy."

"Happy! I could jump out of my skin for joy!" rejoioined Mat.

"If you would make me so likewise!" cried Fanny, "return to the Squire, tell him you have not seen me—say I am absent, ill—say anything, only prevent his coming here."

"I—I wool—I wool; bless you, leave me alone for a bit of a lie!" So saying, Mat hastily departed on his mission to the squire.

"Father I will not disobey you," faltered Fanny; "said I not—'My home shall be my father's hearth, my only thought his happiness?' It shall—it shall. Come, Sophy, come—come!"

---

## CHAP. III.

"The course of strange events no check impedes—
Another to another still succeeds."

ANXIOUS MOMENTS.—THE RIVALS.—I'LL HA' A PEEP AT HIM FROM BE-
HIND THE BUSHES.—THE THREAT.—THE LOUT HAS GONE AT LAST.

"'Sdeath what an age my rustic beauty tarries," exclaimed the squire, who had been anxiously awaiting the arrival of Fanny near the thick clump of trees, a short distance from the farm house; "each moment seems an age to the expectant lover's heart. Lover! pshaw—I am getting senti-

*( To be continued.)*

SHADWELL CASTLE.

# EMELINE;
### OR,
# THE LOVE PLEDGE.

*[Continued from page 8.]*

The music ceased, and with it the vocal strain; but, although Uberto, who, before its conclusion, had aroused from his slumber, looked keenly in every direction to ascertain the person of the songster, no traces of the mysterious being could be seen.

The robber chief overwelmed with doubt and anxiety, now drew his mantle carefully around him, and with agitated steps hastened to make good the appointment he had made with his lieutenant Freeman. A very few minutes of sharp walking brought him near the ruins of the ancient castle of Almanza, whose dark, frowning battlements, betokened the solidity of a mountain. Looking carefully around him on all sides to see that none watched his procedure, the brigand crossed the fosse, passed through the large and antiquated court-yard, and entering the hall, took his station amid fifty of the bravest hearts—that ever boasted of Britain for a birth-place.

Placing some horns upon the huge oaken table, Freeman filled one with canary and presented it to his leader, who rose and, toasting all present, drunk off the ruby liquid.

The example was quickly followed—flagon after flagon disappeared in rapid succession—and blithely the time passed till—

"Slowly sunk the ruddy globe of light,
And o'er the shaded landscape rush'd the night."

At this juncture, Uberto called for silence, which being obtained, he arose from his seat and thus addressed them :—

"Imps of the forest—for so the world call you—I again demand your aid; say, are ye all willing to render it?"

"We are!" was the universal response, each hand grasping the hilt of a dagger.

"I am satisfied!" said Uberto; "Now listen."

"Emeline, the beauteous daughter of Sir Launcelot Shadwell, is this night to celebrate her nativity at Shadwell Castle, near the forest border. All the gentry, for some miles round, are invited to join in the festivities, and among them I shall mingle; but observe what I say—I shall disguise myself in the garb of a monk, and enter the castle. In this disguise I shall have free access, and be enabled, without suspicion, to hold converse with the fair one; be you near to answer my signal, which you will know by a blue-light ascending upwards; assemble near where that light is to be seen, but be not too close together, as you may be suspected. On you, Freeman, must devolve the office of bearing away our fair charge; mount thy best steed, therefore, and be on the drawbridge directly you see the light. I shall convey the maiden thither—seize her, and then—"

"To the cave! the cave!" interrupted Freeman, grimly.

"Shrewdly guessed," rejoined Uberto; "and now, since I am so well understood, perhaps, Freeman, you will be kind enough to array me—for by'r Lady, I am not ingenious enough to be my own valet. The rest of you away to your posts." So saying, Uberto stepped up to an iron chest that was carefully concealed beneath some rubbish, from the interior of which he drew forth the vestments necessary for his assumed office, and in a little time all was adjusted.

They now mounted their steeds and passed quickly through the forest; already had the band taken their several stations, and ever and anon answered their challenge. At length the lofty towers of Shadwell Castle appeared to their view; a thousand flitting lights, like little fairies dancing in the sunbeams, were seen skipping about the antiquated apartments, showing that all was bustle and merriment within.

They now parted, and Uberto, with all possible dignity, galloped into the court-yard. Sir Launcelot, who had a great veneration for the clergy, promptly attended to hold the stirrup, and Uberto, with true clerical dignity, descended from his steed.

"Sir Abbot," said the knight subserviently, "though unknown to me thou art welcome to my castle. By what name shall I introduce thee to my friends?"

"The Abbot Rainsford," replied Uberto, firmly.

"Then, kind sir, you are welcome; walk into our festive hall—I will give direction that due honor be paid the church!"

Taking Uberto's arm within his own, Sir Launcelot conducted him to the hall, where were assembled the first nobles of the land. After the fatigue of introduction had been gone through, the *soi-disant* abbot was lead to a seat, where his wants, as well as those of all present, were speedily attended. Such viands as could not be equalled elsewhere, graced the loaded tables; all were happy, all were gay—for they came to toast the fairest maiden in Britain.

———

## CHAP. III.

" Like a lost guilty wretch I look around
And start at every footstep "
SHAKSPEARE.

### THE SPECTRE.

The joy of all had been kept at its zenith throughout the day; but all mirth is transitory, and pleasures as the poet tells us

" Are like poppies spread;
You seize the flower, its bloom is shed."

The company one by one withdrew from the hall of feasting, to wander either over the castle, or among some of the numerous walks and shrubberies surrounding it. With his mind bent on the accomplishment of his dark purpose, the robber quitted the rest of the gay throng and wandered alone on the terrace that confronted the castle. The sun, which had sunk to rest in magnificence beneath the curtains of the gilded horizon, was now supplaced by the silver rays of the crescent moon, which had arisen in all its regal grandeur

" To walk her weary course"

through heaven's pure concave, surrounded by myriads of beautiful stars. twinkling and shining with lustrous brilliancy, and casting a peculiar gleam on the surrounding scenery.

Uberto, by dint of stretching his tall form over the frowning battlements, occasionally caught a glimpse of his band, evidently expecting with impatience their leader's signal. Ever and anon a polished blade would become visible in the bright moonlight, which objects, upon the moon receding behind a cloud, would again become lost.

The Brigand seated himself on one of the battlements, and gave way to a variety of reflections: he thought—(gentle reader, do not frown—even a robber can think at times)—he thought of days long gone bye—of those he had loved—those he had injured.

"Oh! thou once dear," he exclaimed, as he gazed stedfastly on the pale face of the moon, " bright as yon orb of light, pure as the glittering planets that roll in majesty about it, wast thou. Why hast not thy injuries been avenged? I am awaiting their avengement; yet still going on, still pursuing the same path of guilt; heavier, day by day, is my calendar of evil—still no power intercepts me. Oh Heaven! is there any reality in thy greatness, or is there not? Would that these stones could reply to my query."

"Uberto!" exclaimed a voice, shrill but powerful, " there is—there is !"

"Fiends !" shouted Uberto, " what's that ?"

No answer being returned to this query, the robber started to his feet and looked carefully around him. Nothing, however, could be seen, and he appeared confounded at the strangeness of the circumstance; but he endeavored, by all the casuistry in his power, to convince himself of the fallacy of his vision.

While thus engaged in deceiving himself at the expence of his reason, a tall figure, clad in a long flowing robe of white, stood before him and gazed intently on his features, suddenly rendered pale by fear.

"Who art thou?" said Uberto sternly, "that wanderest forth from the darksome grave at this hour? Speak! devil—fiend—imp, or whatever thou art," at the same time grasping with a firm hand his sword, which was carefully concealed beneath his monkish habiliments.

"Thine accuser! Lord Alfred of Almanza," answered the figure, and its eyes glared fearfully on the robber as he stood tremblingly before it.

"Lord Alfred of Almanza!" said Uberto, marvelling; "how knowest thou that? Speak!"

"No more shall I deign to tell thee," said the figure, still gazing upon him intently. "Oft have I warned thee, but this, this is the last time. Uberto, Abbot of Rainsford, or whatever *nom-de-guerre* thou thinkest fit to adopt, *beware*! for now the reality of an eternal avenger will be plain, even to such a doubter as thou art."

"Oh, spirit! withhold thy dreadful prophecy," said Uberto, falling against the rampart wall; "whatever be my fate, with resolution shall it be met, but stay your ominous predictions, and spare the wretched."

He ceased—more he would have said, but his tongue refused its office; a tremor come over his whole frame, and, overcome by the glaring, fiery glance that met his gaze whichever way he turned, he raised his hand convulsively to his brow. There he kept it a moment or two, until ashamed of his weakness, and his judgment getting the better of his fear, he, with a violent effort, raised himself from his recumbent posture and boldly advanced, sword-in-hand, determined to face his unearthly opponent. The moon being hidden beneath a cloud, for a time Uberto could see nothing but the dark frowning battlements close to him; at length upon the hidden luminary making her re-appearance in the heavens, he peered carefully around him, but the figure that so lately alarmed him was gone.

The brigand, whose courage returned with the absence of the figure, now sought carefully along the bastioned walks of the terrace, but his search was attended with no success. He now thought it prudent to retrace his steps; besides, his former project called for his immediate attention. Wrapping his huge gown closer round him, and pulling the cowl closely over his face, the robber was soon among the crowd assembled on the lawn. Having arrived thither, he was informed that Sir Launcelot had been very anxious in his enquiries respecting him, and, moreover, wished to see him in the company of his daughter.

"I will comply, instantly," said the *soi-disant* abbot, inwardly exulting that such an opportunity had arrived, and immediately made the best of his way to the hall. He soon found the object of his search. Going up to him, therefore, he, in a firm voice, exclaimed "Sir Launcelot!"

The knight, with a degreee of marked courtesy, returned the salute of recognition, and said—

"My Lord Abbot, I feared thou hadst, from some cause unknown to me, taken offence, and departed without even bestowing thy benedicite on the dwelling of the most obedient servant the Church ever had."

"Pardon my absence," said Uberto, with mock gravity, "but mine is a holy office; it would ill become me to join the gay and laughing throng —pleasure must not deprive my mind of those religious thoughts I ought

*(To be continued.)*

# GARDEN OF ROMANCE.

## FANNY GREENWELL;

### OR,

### THE OLD FARM HOUSE.

*[Continued from our last.]*

mental, and yet 'twere falsehood to deny the term.  Dear Fanny, why did not fate design thee for a higher state?   Why did it place the obstacle of birth between me and bliss?   Pshaw! that can be surmounted, and yet to wrong her innocent confidence!   Duty tells me I ought to break this ill-placed affection, but my heart rebels against it.   Ah! here comes my rustic rival!"

"Yes, I'll take thy advice, George Rutly, and who knows but I may be as lucky as thou be?" ejaculated Michael Wright, the youth spoken of by Sophy as an aspirant to the hand of Fanny, and who had now reached the very spot chosen by the squire as the scene of his assignation; "I'll ax Greenwell to gi' me his daughter for a wife!" he continued, "though I could never find the heart to tell her how dearly I love her, she be so rattlesome and fly-away like; but her sister Sophy guessed as much, and when she jested me, I couldn't for my soul deny it—and why should a man deny that which be his pride?   Yes, I'll do it, I'll put the question to Farmer."   At this moment he discovered the Squire standing near him.  "Eh, the Squire!—Sarvent, Squire!" he said.

"Ah, Michael! what going to be married, eh?" rejoined the Squire.

"Surely he didn't overhear me," thought Michael.   "Why yes—yes, Squire"—he replied.   "I hope—I—"

"I give you joy," said the Squire, sarcastically.

"Thank'ee, Squire, time enough for that when I ha' found the bride."

"Found the bride," echoed the other, "'tis strange to publish the banns without the spinster's name—at church surely I heard the name of Michael Wright among the candidates for matrimonial happiness."

No. 3.

" No you didn't" said Michael " I wish'ee did ;—there's no such luck as yet. You might ha' heard the name o' Wright, but then it warnt Michael, but Peter, cousin Peter. Ah ! he's a happy lad—he's going to be tacked to Bessy Brown, she's a good and a tidy lass and I'm sure, from the bottom of my heart, I wish 'em happy."

" Peter was it?" said the Squire, " I thought it sounded very like Michael. How is it, Michael, that your cousin is more successful with our village beauties than yourself?"

" Oh, drat him, it's all along o' his feace."

" His face ! surely *that* can't befriend him much," sneered the Squire ; " for to say the truth, he's rather ill-favored."

" I've often told him he's as ugly as sin compared wi' me," said Michael, " but what's the use of a pretty feace if thee ha' na' some brass in it ? I tell him his feace 'ud look parson out o' his tithes at any time, and I'll be whipped if it wouldn't."

" Sdeath !" muttered the Squire, aside, " can that lout, Mat Maythorn, have delivered my message ? If so, what mischance prevents her coming ? Perhaps she has observed Michael and wishes his absence.—Good day, Michael ;" said he, at the same time looking anxiously toward the old farm house.

" What the dickens be he straining his neck as long as a gander's for, I wonder?" muttered Michael ; " he be waiting for somebody, that's cartain—I'll make believe to go, creep round by the bank, and ha' a peep at him from behind bushes."

" No traces of her yet," said the Squire, soliloquising.

" Her ! he said her—then it's a petticoat as sure as ninepence," said Michael. " They do say he ha' cast an eye on Fanny ; woe be to him if he has a thought o' wrong towards her, although he be a Squire, that shouldn't save him ; dang me if I wouldn't break his back like a baccapipe. Dutiful good day, Squire," he exclaimed loudly, and immediately took his departure, muttering as he went, " If it be Fanny Greenwell, d— me, but I'll spoil his poaching."

" The lout has gone at last," ejaculated the Squire ; " the village gossips say that he aspires to the hand of Fanny—the charming, timid Fanny. No, no, young Plough and Harrow, my blooming rose must not be worn by thee. Death and the devil ! I'm losing all patience ; the fidgets are consuming me.—Ah, here comes Mat, but where's Fanny ? She does not accompany him."

" Pheugh ! aint I made smart haste?" cried Mat Maythorn, rushing up to the squire.

" Haste, you snail ! Tell me did you see her?" rejoined the other hastily.

" Yes !"

" And what said she ?"

" What did she say ? oh, I'm ashamed to tell you, squire, it's so unlike a lady !"

" Out with it," said the Squire impatiently.

" You really must excuse me."

" I will not, sirrah—what said she ?"

" Oh, well, if you wish, she said, ' there were my betters not far a field and I might go to the devil.' "

" What, Fanny Greenwell ?"

" No, Beckey Wibbles !"

" Curse Beckey Wibbles !" roared the Squire.

" Moreover, she said—"

" What, Fanny ?" interrupted the Squire.

" No, Beckey !" said Mat coolly.

" You rascal !" thundered the Squire, shaking his whip menacingly ; " if you don't instantly discharge your mission, I'll—"

" Will you though ?" said Mat, " is that the way you usually pay your postmen ? He be but a snipe of a fellow," thought Mat, " I'll give him a challenge. I say, squire !" he cried ; " if I may be so bold, just for fun loike, or if thee like it better, I'll wrastle thee for a mug o' ale—come on !"

" Fool !" shrieked the squire, " what of Fanny ?"

" Ecod, how troubled thee beest about her," said Mat ; " aye, it's nat'-ral—just like me and Beckey Wibbles !"

" I lose all patience," growled the other. " Mat !" he continued, " tell your story straight forward, and I'll give you a guinea !"

" Will 'ee ? say it agin."

" I repeat it," said the squire.

" Lard ! a goulden guinea—tip him over, Squire, and I'll tell'e all."

The Squire having tendered the proffered guerdon, Mat commenced :—

" First and foremost, I meets you here—"

" Never mind that," said the Squire.

" Oh, but I did," said mat, " or how could I do the job tidily. And you says to me, ' Mat,' says you, ' Mat,'—you were very familiar Squire—"

" Pshaw !"

" Mat," says you, " do thou go down to the Briars, and watch a 'tu-nity to speak to Miss Fanny Greenwell all alone ; wi' nobody but herself."

" You did this ?"

" No, I didn't—but stop a bit ; I must tell my story my own way."

" Do so and speedily !" said the Squire ; " quick !—quick !—haste I say !"

" Did'nt I make haste? So I was to tell Miss Greenwell, Squire were waiting to speak wi' her at the end o' the copse."

" That's correct."

" I'm 'shamed of thee," said Mat, " it be unmannerly to interrupt. But you see I hadn't got further on the road than the stile, and sure enough there she wur !"

" What Fanny ?"

" No, Beckey Wibbles, but we won't mind her now ; I didn't much, so I kept on telling over the message in my mind, for fear I might forget—then I came to the Briar's shed ; she'd got a letter in her hand—"

" For me ?" asked the Squire.

" No, for Jemmy Jenkins !" replied Mat.

" Pshaw !" growled the Squire.

" Lard, lard, how the petticoats do bother a body!" ejaculated Mat. " Well I came to Greenwell's farm, and there she was—"

" Whom?"

" Miss Sophy and Fa——. I'm bothered, how shall I twist un round?" thought Mat, breaking off short at the word ' Fanny.'

" Sophy and Fanny ?" said the Squire, enquiringly.

" Yes—no—that is—"

Again the rustic seemed at a loss for a reply.   " What the dickens can the Squire wan't with a farmer's daughter," thought he.   " I'll tell him the truth, and then perhaps he won't mislist the lass any more," he muttered.

" Yes, Squire, there they were, Sophy and Fanny ; so what does I do first, but up and tells 'em all about Beckey Wibbles and her wollytine ; then they said Wollytine's day be in February, and this be in August, so it could'nt be a wollytine at all you see, and I wur quite pleasured.  Then says I to Miss Fanny—"

" To Fanny—go on."

" Yes—there be somebody waiting for 'ee down at the copse, Miss," said I.   ' Whom ?' said she, in a whisper.   ' Young Squire,' said I.  ' The Squire ?' says she."

" Delighted, no doubt," interrupted the Squire.

" No she warnt.—' Tell the Squire,' says she—and I never seed her look so black in all my born days—' Tell him, friend Mathew,' says she, and then her eyes twinkled so pretty—' tell him that I be going to take tea this arternoon.—tell him I am absent—I'm ill—I've got a hollow stump, and I be going to have him lugged out in a crack,' and arter that, says she, ' I have a nasty toad of a corn, and I'll have him cut at the same time.' "

" There must be some meaning in this," muttered the Squire, in a tone too low for the sound to meet Mat's ear, " she never could send so confused a reply : perhaps accident prevents her coming, and she has given an evasive answer to this lout to avoid suspicion.  It is well I am prepared," he continued, drawing a pocket-book from his vest, and taking a letter therefrom ; " If she has scruples, this will remove them all.  Mathew !"

" Mathew ! not Mat—here is something particular to do," thought the rustic.   " Squire," he replied.

" Return to the Briar's Farm ; contrive to see Miss Fanny Greenwell alone—mind, *alone*, and unobserved.   Give her this letter ; I feel assured some unforeseen circumstance prevents her coming—and when done meet me on the lawn at the Hall, and another guinea shall be yours."

" What ! another.   Huzza ! huzza !" cried Mat.   " That be the sort of work—two guineas ! I'll ha' a new pair o' buckskins—long life to the Squire.   I'll gi' the letter, and be back in no time !'

" Yes, it must be so," ejaculated the Squire, " Fanny would never send so rude an answer ; at all hazards, that letter will bring her to the appointed spot.   Yes, Fanny, thy image is graven upon my heart, and the world has no charms unless thou share it with me !"

" Mighty foine, share it with *thee*," said Michael Wright, emerging from his place of concealment behind the bushes ; " I'll take care she don't though.   As to that fetch-and-carry fellow, Mat, I'll ha' a crow to pick wi' he.   Ah, Fanny ! where be thy heart ; thou canst smile upon the deceiver, yet scorn to welcome him that means thee honest ?   But d——me if I despair though—she be young, and girls be always

*( To be continued.)*

CALTHART

# EMELINE;
### OR,
## THE LOVE PLEDGE.

*[Continued from page* 16.]

to possess. I therefore wandered on the terrace that overlooks the plain in front of this castle, and gave way for a time to reflection."

" Ah !" said the knight, with astonishment," that terrace is said to be haunted. I dare say, though, you met with no interruption from anything unearthly ?"

" No !" answered Uberto, shuddering as he denied the fact of his late interview with the spectre, " nor should I be inclined to place much faith in the veracity of those who circulated such a report."

" I believe it, however, to be a fact," returned the knight ; " besides, I have ofttimes heard the most beautiful music as I have passed the battlements by night. I have had that part of the castle strictly searched, but never gained any clue to the existence of any thing human ; how to account for it, therefore, in any other way than I have, I know not."

" It is strange," muttered Uberto, " but more of this anon. Where is thy daughter ?"

" Let us seek her," replied the knight : and drawing the arm of the brigand within his own, they started off in pursuit of their project.

## CHAP. IV.

> " 'Twas blow for blow, disputed inch by inch—
> For one would not retreat, nor 'tother flinch."—*Byron.*

### THE LOVE PLEDGE.

A great portion of the company had now quitted the castle, and the tumultuous preparations of the day had yielded to the soft stillness of evening, when the young knight, Calthart Burgoyne, sallied forth from his villa to meet his heart's dearest treasure, the lovely Emeline.

The gardens of Shadwell were delightfully interspersed with groves of lilac and citron, which, agitated by a gentle breeze, spread around a delightful odour, At their eastern extremity was erected a splendid pavilion, at the back of which, was the remains of an ancient grotto. Here,

> " When the fair moon's refulgent lamp of night,
> O'er heaven's pure azure spreads her sacred light,"

the lovers would meet, and, unseen by mortal eye, breathe forth the sentiments of their hearts. It was such an evening as this, that closed the sports at the castle at the time of which we write. Not a cloud was to be seen, when Calthart proceeding to the well-known spot, a female of enchanting beauty rushed into his fond embrace, and for a few moments the lovers regarded each other with all the ardour of mutual affection.

"Oh, this is indeed, bliss," cried Calthart, gently untwining his arm from around the lovely maid; "to hold thee in these arms, and call thee mine. But why that tear, my beloved?" and he kissed the pearly intruder from her cheek.

"Alas! I know not why, my Calthart," said Emeline, "but a mysterious dread rushes through my frame, as though some fearful and uncontrollable calamity were about to happen."

"Nay, heed it not, my love," cried Calthart, folding the trembler to his breast, " 'tis but the excitement of your imagination, which you must strive to conquer."

"I will do so," returned Emeline; "but look—what is that?" at the same time directing his attention to a dark object a short distance before her.

"Oh, 'tis but the shadow of some neighboring tree, waved by the passing breeze," "said Calthart; "and yet it cannot be—no, by heaven, 'tis some vile spy," and, grasping his faulchion, he rushed to the spot; but the person as quickly retreated, though not before he had a full view of his retiring figure.

"That gigantic figure bespeaks it Hugh Cuthlin, or I am much deceived."

"Hugh Cuthlin !" echoed Emeline, clinging to her lover, and terror blanching her fair cheeks; "gracious powers, why comes he here?"

"That I should have asked him," exclaimed Calthart, "had he not, like a craven, fled. But why this agitation? What has occured, coupled with that name, to occasion this emotion? Tell me, I conjure thee."

"Listen," cried the still trembling Emeline, "and I will explain all Thou art aware Hugh Cuthlin was the early suitor for my hand; thou also knowest that my father, yeilding to my repeated entreaties, desired him, upon plea of my extreme youth, to withdraw his suit, and never again visit the castle. With joy I found myself freed from his detested proposals, and, as I hoped, for ever; but in this I was deceived, for but a short time elapsed ere he again appeared, and renewed his pretensions with all their former ardor. But he was again rejected, and vain were his efforts to conceal his rage at this second refusal, which he vehemently averred arose from my love for some more favored rival.

"'Nay, deny it not,' he cried, as he observed me about to interrupt him, 'I know the presumptuous stripling who is about to cross my wishes, but let him beware, for Hugh Cuthlin is his deadly foe;' and with these words he left me. From that time his conduct became entirely changed: that animated and ardent expression, which had till now illumined his features whenever we met, was supplanted by a gloomy scowl, and he would fix his large dark eyes upon my face with an indescribable and fierce intensity that filled me with dismay. This morning I abruptly met him near this grot; fire seemed to flash from his eyes. With difficulty could I suppress an ejaculation of terror, as I turned to avoid him; but seizing my arm, he exclaimed, 'The time will soon come, when Emeline shall have cause to repent the rejection of Hugh Cuthlin. Think not, proud girl, ever to become the bride of Calthart; no, I swear rather than that, my dagger should stretch thee lifeless at my feet. Never shall the boy, Calthart, triumph over Hugh Cuthlin!' and throwing me rudely from him, with the word 'remember,' rushed from my sight. It was the recollection of these dreadful words, coupled with his sudden appearance, that occasioned my terror. I am convinced he has a heart black enough to carry his threat into execution; but, avoid him, Calthart, as you would a pestilence, for should you meet, I tremble for the consequences."

"Nay, fear it not, my beloved."

The sound of distant footsteps now broke on the surrounding stillness, and, "Emeline!" borne on the gentle breeze, reached their ears. This was an unwelcome sound to the lovers, as it was evidently some person seeking the maiden, who instantly arose.

"I will meet you again in an hour," said she; "for the present, farewell!"

"Farewell, my love," returned he, folding her to his bosom. "In an hour, and at this place, we meet again; till then, farewell."

For a moment their lips met, then sighing, they tore themselves away from each other. Calthart followed her with his eyes, until the closing of a small postern, that led to an enclosed spot of ground at the back of the pavilion, hid her from his view; then drawing his cloak around him, he mused on the threatening words uttered by Hugh Cuthlin. Lost in these reflections, he proceeded forward, heedless of the surrounding objects, until a sudden exclamation startled him; when, on looking towards the spot from whence the sounds proceeded, he again beheld the same figure which he had seen in the grotto, who was slowly preceding him, apparently unconscious of being observed. The hot blood rushed to the cheeks of Calthart, and his proud heart swelled to repay the insult offered to his beloved, and hastening forward, the next moment beheld him at the side of the object of his resentment. Hugh Cuthlin started at his sudden appearance, but there was a storm gathering in those dark penetrating eyes, as he fixed them on the intruder, that would have appalled the heart of any one less bold than Calthart, who returning his scathing glance with one of scorn, exclaimed—

"Nay, reserve thy fierce looks, man, for one who fears them; methinks they sit but ill on the features of a mean listener, and *one* who, on discovery, fled, like a vile caitiff as he was."

"By heaven, 'tis false," vociferated Hugh Cuthlin, with fury; "'twas chance alone that led me to that spot, which I as quickly quitted; but," added he, with a galling sneer, "'twas not through fear of *thee*."

"And was it *chance* that kept thee there till now?" returned Calthart.

"Peace, babbler as thou art," interrupted the other, "or not even thy immeasurable inferiority shall save thee from the chastisement thou so richly deserve."

"'Twas *nobly* spoken," returned Calthart, with cutting irony, "and well befits the being who would rather utter his threats in the ear of a defenceless maid, than face the object of his resentment as a man."

"Detested slave, I'll hear no more," vociferated Hugh Cuthlin, franticly grasping his sabre; "that falsehood shall be refuted."

"Now I understand thee," dauntlessly exclaimed Calthart," and my answer is in my scabbard."

"Then pluck it forth, and see if thou canst guard thy life."

"Nay look to thine own," returned Calthart, as his bright blade gleamed in the air.

The cloaks of the combatants had fallen off, and the contrast in their appearance was strikingly evident. Calthart stood a model of manly symmetry, while his opponent seemed like a second Hercules, the gigantic proportions of his limbs indicating strength nearly superhuman. A look of defiance flashed from the eyes of each; that of Hugh Cuthlin had in it the malice of a fiend, while Calthart's was one of determined courage. Hugh rushed to the onset with the ferocity of a tiger, but Calthart received him with unshrinking valour, that bade defiance to his efforts, until roused to madness by the coolness displayed by his antagonist, Hugh Cuthlin grasped his ponderous weapon; with both hands he raised it high above his head; descending, it cleft the air, but Calthart, stepping aside, avoided the stroke, and ere Hugh Cuthlin could recover himself, he, by a sideblow, laid him prostrate on the earth; then, placing his foot upon his broad chest, he bade him ask his life.

"Never!" exclaimed the other, in accents scarcely audible from passion, "strike! the pangs of death are less bitter than those I now feel."

"Calthart, taking his foot from his body, cried—

"No, Hugh Cuthlin, 'tis enough; I do not want thy life. Take it, and endeavor to forget the occurrence of the evening, as I shall,"

For a few moments Hugh Cuthlin seemed scarcely to believe his senses; then starting to his feet, revenge, like that of a demon, raging in his breast, and crushing every nobler feeling.

"Forget my base defeat!" he cried, in a voice hoarse and convulsed,— "never! 'twere easier to forget myself. No, revenge is still within my power, and like lightning shall it fall on thy detested head," and he rushed frantic from the spot.

An hour had now passed away, and Calthart hastened to keep his appointment at the grotto. On reaching it, however, Emeline was not there. This, at first, surprised him, but concluding something unavoidable had occurred to detain her, he entered the ruins with the intention of waiting;

*(To be continued.)*

# GARDEN OF ROMANCE.

## FANNY GREENWELL;
### OR,
### THE OLD FARM HOUSE.

*[Continued from our last.]*

dazzled wi' foine clothes and flowery speeches—I'll seek her feyther, and tell him all. No, no, time enough; my first care must be, if I can, to prevent their meeting. Ah, Squire, thee mayst be a cute un, but thee hast only another to out-wit besides me, and that's Old Nick! Drat thee, I'll watch thee well!" So saying, the rejected lover rushed hastily from the spot.

### CHAP. IV.

> "Ah me, how weak a thing
> The heart of woman is."—*Julius Cæsar.*

THE OLD FARM HOUSE—THERE'S A GUINEA'S WORTH—DISCOVERY OF
THE LETTER—WHERE'S FANNY?—GONE!—GONE!

Our readers must now accompany us to the interior of the kitchen, or common sitting room of the Briar's Farm. The exterior of its large window (which was now thrown open) was beautifully ornamented with flowering shrubs that loaded the pure air with a delightful fragrance. Near this stood a huge oaken arm-chair, upon which Fanny Greenwell threw herself, after having sent what appeared to the Squire so singular a message.

"Happy—happy Sophy," said she, abstractedly, "thou art content with the—the husband of thy choice—thou art blessed by a fond father's sanction, and your lot in life will be happy—when, oh when, will the

No. 4.

prospect of such a day dawn on me ?   Thou hast no ambition—no yearning beyond thy humble state ; while I—Fate was a juggler when she gave the farmer a second child—she was meant for a blessing, but cast in a higher mould, endowed with a heart above the dull drudgery of a farm or the love of green fields.   No, fancy ever pictured the bustle of the gay world— of routes, of balls, the scene of bright variety.   Why do I think of them ?   I but deceive myself—they were never meant for me ; and yet Melville has often sworn that I should see them yet, as his wife ; and yet my father would crush the prospects of his child.   Ah ! fear not my father, your daughter knows her duty and never will forget it—anything but his wife she will never become, and he has called Heaven to witness.   I believed him—I—I—believe him still."

Upon reaching the farm-house, Mat Maythorn gently opened the door. " Fanny—Miss Fanny !" he whispered.

" Who's there ?" cried Fanny.

" Nobody, only I, Mat Maythorn, miss.   Here's a letter for you—there's a guinea's worth," said he, placing the note in the hand of Fanny.

" What ?" said Fanny.

" Pshaw ! I mean it's worth a guinea to me," rejoined Mat, "and I warrant when you read it you wouldn't take two ; it's from the Squire."

" Shall I reject it ?   Yet why should I ?" thought Fanny.   " The caprice of my father may prevent me seeing him, but it cannot be criminal to hear that he is well and happy ?"

" I'll be off to the Hall," cried Mat.   " Who'll say I didn't manage that clever ?   That's because Becky Wibbles warn't sitting a top o' the style.   Good bye, Miss Fanny, I must hurry back, or I shall miss the fun at the harvest home.   Good bye."

" My hand trembles—I dread, yet wish to read it," said Fanny, pressing the note to her lips.   " Let me be careful no one observes me," she continued, as, looking cautiously around her, she broke the seal.   " Yes," 'tis his hand ; on colored paper too—how unlike to any here."

Again she looked about her as though to convince herself no one was near ; at length, becoming satisfied there was no cause for alarm, she unfolded the letter, and read as follows :—

" My own dear Fanny, I have prepared this letter in case accident should prevent me the happiness of your presence at the appointed spot. You already know the fate that threatens me, it is in your power alone to prevent it.   Pity me, Fanny ; let not the avarice of my father—who would have me wed one I hate—for ever blight my peace.   If, as you have often said, you love me, prove it now—the Rev. Mr. Mortimer waits at the Hall with a special license to make me the happiest of men ; it is in your power by refusal to render me the most wretched ; deny me and obedience to my father's will hurries me to London, to unite my destiny to a being I must ever loathe.

Yours ever,<br>MELVILLE."

How shall I act ? how decide ?" ejaculated Fanny ; " no friend—no adviser—divided passions are warring in my soul—the home of infancy, my sister, father, the partners of my early life bid me stay ; but there is a voice that soundeth sweeter far—it is his, my first, my only love ; he invites me to a higher and a happier fate! Why should I not fly to meet its round of joy? but that sorrow kills that joy, for I hear a father's bitter sigh, I see a fond girl's tear!—Sigh not father—weep not sister—Fanny will dwell here for ever."

This resolve, was, however, soon broken. Glancing once more on that part of the note which run: " It is in your power to render me the most wretched," she cried, " in my power, Melville? Oh, happy, doubly happy be each moment of your life, shall ever be my prayer!" Again she read —" to unite my destiny, to a being I must ever loathe." " For me, for me he would brave even a father's anger! and yet I fear to meet mine, and by delay consign to misery the heart that loves me! What says he— ' the minister is at the Hall to make me his for ever!' I cannot pause —no father's fear—no sister's caprice must stay me. Yes, Melville, I will be thine—thine—you have called Heaven to witness your truth, and ungenerous would be my heart to doubt it; when united, we will return, and smiles of joy shall welcome Fanny as the Squire's bride!"

" What we wish to be true, we are apt to believe," saith the proverb. Thus it was with Fanny, who, judging all hearts by the purity of her own, little recked

" That man to man so oft unjust,
Is always so to woman;"

and placed the most implicit faith on every asseveration the Squire breathed.

" I will preserve this paper to the latest hour of my life!" said she, placing the letter in a bureau, which she locked; and hastily snatching her hat from the door, was about to rush from the farm house. The door was, however, thrown back by some one on the outside, and the next moment Sophy entered.

" Why Fanny, whither are you going?" cried she.

" I—I—I am faint—the evening is hot and sultry—my—my heart throbs, and my brain burns," faltered Fanny, bursting into a passion of tears. " I—I want air—air," and she fell half fainting into her sister's arms.

" Fanny, dear Fanny, what wildness is this?" said Sophy. " Thy eyes are streaming with tears! Cheer, cheer thee, dear sister. You will be better soon—tears lighten the heart; come, you brighten—that's right, that's brave now. Fanny, am I unworthy your love? Tell me what has occasioned this?"

Fanny, who well knew that to unravel her design of meeting the Squire would be the means of its prevention, after a pause, said :—

" This solitude, this setting gloom—for see, the sun has sunk below the trees, all is death-like still—I—I am not used to be alone, and sad and dull thoughts will come at times, even to the happiest. Fancy conjured up a thousand forms—fear was resting on my heart; you came, dear Sophy, and I joy, for fear has fled."

" The pure fresh air will revive you," said Sophy; I will be your companion—come!"

" No, no, I need no companion," replied Fanny. " See, my father comes, and with him, one to thee most dear. By our love, Sophy, do not mention what has past. I will return speedily to share the sports that will gladden all,   Adieu !   Now Melville, I fly to save you from the fate you deem so wretched," she ejaculated, inwardly, as with hurried steps she quitted her father's roof.

" Strange, romantic girl!" said Sophy, gazing after her, I do not wonder at thy melancholy, for this is a dreary abode when the twilight sets ; but here comes George and my father to kill its gloom."

" Here is your treasure, George," said Greenwell, as he entered—" so good, so dutiful a child cannot fail to ensure you happiness ; there is a lurking round my heart that would fain prompt me to deny her to thee, but Heaven forbid that my selfishness should be the bar between the hearts that love sincerely.   Take her, George ; she will be to thee what she has ever been to me—a blessing !"

" Ah, sir, you need not extol her virtues, my heart has long known and prized them ;" said George.   " Do not blush, Sophy," he continued, " the cheek may crimson at untruth, but should never color at the praise that is just."

" Come, come, no more compliments," interrupted Greenwell, " we have other and more pleasing work ; it is to make happy those honest hearts whose toil doth fill the merchant's granary ; this is the last day of harvest and it has been a bright one.   Heaven ever keep it so, for the sake of the poor and needy.   Sophy, order Joe and Robert to bring hither the barrel of ale I told them—this night we devote to glee."

Upon hearing this order, George smiled.

" You doubtless wonder at my precaution, George," remarked Greenwell, " but among the lads are some dry souls, and I would fain keep the head cool, that the heels may be light."

" A wise resolve, sir," said George.

" From this casement," resumed Greenwell, " we may enjoy their rustic sports ; good servants should always find good masters ; and the wheat no sooner springs from the earth than the rogues talk of this day as the end of their labor, and one of the happiest of their lives.   The blessing of Heaven has been with me, George ; I have gained respect, competence, and, I trust, not undeservedly."

" Do they not assemble early, sir ?" asked George, who now heard the sound of music from without.

" No," returned Greenwell, " the day is past, and they are anxious for the dance.   But, as I was about to tell you, the world has thriven with me ; a short time since I purchased the lease of Gap-farm—your name shall be transferred to it in place of mine ; I cannot give you a better proof how I estimate your industry than in bestowing it as a portion for my Sophy, and perhaps her children, you young dog."

So saying, he gave George a hearty nudge and approached the bureau.

" I have it here," he exclaimed, " but in which drawer I placed it, hang me if I can tell !"

Taking a key from his pocket he opened the very drawer in which Fanny had deposited her letter from Squire Melville.

" No it's not in this one—Ah ! what's this ?  ' To Miss Francis Greenwell !' on gaudy paper too," cried the farmer ; " be still my heart —Hell !  wake not a father's fears,  What ails my sight—my frame ? every nerve doth tremble."

*( To be continued. )*

# EMELINE;

OR,

# THE LOVE PLEDGE.

[*Continued from page 24.*]

but scarcely had he seated himself for that purpose on one of the overthrown pillars, when a confused noise, but a short distance from him, struck on his ear. He sprung to his feet, and on so doing, kicked against something on the ground, which on taking up proved to be a bracelet, which he instantly recognised, and exclaimed—

" 'Tis Emeline's !"

Hardly had the words escaped his lips, ere the noise was again repeated, and, " Calthart, save me, save me !" was uttered by a voice, the first tones of which thrilled to his heart.

" Save thee !" thundered a horse voice, as Calthart rushed forward," no power on earth shall save thee," and the shriek that followed curdled the blood in his veins, and rooted him to the spot.

At this instant a dark figure glided past; he sprung forward and seized it, but the treacherous cloak alone remained in his grasp. A low moan, and his own name faintly repeated, now broke upon his ear.

" Ha !" I come, I come," exclaimed he, franticly rushing towards the spot; but madness seized upon his brain as he beheld at his feet the body of her he loved more than all created beings. A heavenly smile played around her coral lips, from between which the breath had just issued in . ejaculating the name of that being who now stood gazing at her. He moved not, no sound escaped him; he stood as though some deadly blow had palsied every faculty, a slight tremor afflicted his frame, and his breast heaved convulsively :—

" Emeline," burst in hysteric accents from his aching heart, his eyeballs glared wildly around; at length they became fixed on the body, and a dreadful presentiment crossed his mind.

At this moment he beheld something on the ground; he eagerly seized it—it was a dagger, encrusted with blood.

" 'Tis Emeline's blood !" he exclaimed, in a convulsed voice, and was about to dash the weapon to the ground, when he observed some letters on the blade—'twas the name of his deadly rival.

" Oh, heartless villain, is this the return for the life I gave thee ?" exclaimed he, furiously; " but thou hast not yet escaped me, nor shalt thou, for even now, I come to cleave thee to the dust."

So saying, he thrust the dagger between the folds of his garment, and was on the point of rushing from the spot, when the maiden who lay by his side, as he supposed, murdered, opened her soft blue eyes, and mildly ejaculated—" Calthart !"

The sound acted like an electric shock on the young knight, who, raising her gently on his arm, exclaimed—

" What mystery is this ? But a moment since thou wert laying on the cold earth apparently lifeless; a dagger by your side encrusted with blood, on the hilt of which is engraved the name of my hated rival—Hugh Cuthlin !"

" 'Tis the monster's own blood !" said Emeline; " but come, love—I am still very faint and weak ; let us, therefore, once more retire to the grot, and when my strength is a little recruited all shall be explained."

A kiss, was all the reply to this request, but drawing the arm of the maiden tenderly within his own, Calthart conducted her slowly towards the grot.

The moon, which for the last few seconds had been veiled beneath a dark cloud, now burst her black fetters, and shone forth with almost inconceivable splendor, smiling as it were on the procedure of the young lovers, as they passed beneath its silvery rays, and sought a shelter in the grot before described. Arrived thither, they seated themselves. For a time, however, not a word passed betwen them ; at last the silence was broken by Emeline, who said—

Calthart, I am now much restored, and will relate the strange occurrences that have so lately befallen me."

" Which I am all anxiety to learn," replied Calthart.

Emeline commenced. " Upon proceeding to the place of redezvous at the time appointed, I was intercepted by the villain Hugh Cuthlin. I stept out of the way, and endeavored to shun him ; the effort was, however, a vain one, for the next moment I found myself within the ruffian's grasp. He had seized me roughly by the arm, and drawing from beneath the folds of his huge cloak a short dagger, was about to—"

" What !" gasped Calthart.

" Plunge it into my bosom," returned the maiden ; " but I uttered a loud shriek for help, when a figure of the same gigantic stature as that of Hugh Cuthlin, rushed to the spot, at the very moment the upraised dagger glimmered in the air."

" What then occurred ;" demanded Calthart.

" With giant-like strength, the stranger seized the uplifted arm of my persecutor, and wresting the dagger from the monster's grasp, at the same time shouting in a tone of exultation, " Traitor, receive thy reward," plunged it into his bosom, but instately withdrew it and dashed it to the ground. Although thus wounded, Hugh Cuthlin, giving utterance to an awful imprecation, rushed precipitately from the spot. What happened afterwards, or what became of my kind protector, I cannot say ; the excessive emotion caused by the brutal attack upon my life, proved too much for me to bear—my head became giddy— and, giving utterance to thy name, I fell swooning to the earth—in which situation you discovered me.

" Thank Heaven, matters are no worse," ejaculated Calthart, drawing the fair one closer to his bosom.

A long silence was again observed between them, which, as before, was broken by the maiden—who exclaimed :—

" Why art *thou* so pensive, Calthart ?"

The youth replied :—

" Your pardon, lady—I was, for a moment, lost in admiration of yon fair and shining moon—how calm, how beautiful she sails through the bright blue heavens, like a silver galley laden with charms to soothe the world. She smooths the troubled ocean, burnishes the rough face of earth, chastens the hot langour of the Indian air, and stills the arrowy bluster of the north. She seems to whisper consolation in the ears of drooping flowers, and wakes a thousand torpid rivers into sparkling life by her enchanting smile !—Emeline, thou art that magic moon—as bright, as chaste, as wonderful—the rivers are thy countless suitors—the flowers their trembling love !"

" Fye—thou art a flatterer; and like all flatterers, thou dost magnify the object of thy praise, till e'en itself knows not its own image; as the curved mirror shows to the gazer a distorted picture."

" Nay, sweet Emeline, by that moon, and by thyself, I swear—sure nature ne'er created chaster seals to a true oath—1 swear, the rivers of a thousand noble hearts are tided by thy smile, and ebb and flow by thy bright influence—my own heart vouches it; but ah ! I feel, whilst thou dost sway all streams, and animate all hopes as well as mine, still there is but one moon, one cheering light in the vast universe for me."

" Go to," said Emeline, "I ought to chide thee, but I know not how, and would not learn the way. I love the moon for her sweet light, and the repose with which she fills the world ; but as an emblem, she befits not me, for she is cold, and proud, and lonely amid the crowded stars that sparkle around her—she walks a regal way, costly and royal, even in her charity; for she scatters gems to the humblest shrubs, and creams the obedient sea with liquid silver. Yes, 'tis a solemn awful sway she holds, restless and changing ever—without a mate—almost without a home. See'st thou yon tiny twinkling starlet tracking her course—bright in its borrowed light—meek in its pretensions—with scarce one value, save its constancy ?—Such am I, if I do know myself; if not, such is my loftiest ambition."

"Thou art—thou art—my star of hope—of destiny---of glory; my morning star, awakening adoration ; my evening star of peace---my guide star when away---the fixed star that shall hallow my grave---"

" Peace, Calthart."

" Would I might say, the star to beam content upon my future home."

" Be assured---I have plighted thee my faith, and thou shalt find I will redeem, with a wife's fondness, all that a maiden's lip hath uttered. But here, my Calthart," continued Emeline, at the same time taking a small miniature from her bosom, and presenting it to the young knight, " this ---this shall be the pledge; take it, therefore, as a guerdon of my love, until it's beyond the power of mortals to separate us."

" Thanks, thanks ! my dear Emeline," said Calthart, while a bright tear trickled down his healthful cheeks; " this shall, indeed, be a pledge---of love---of truth---of constancy---a pledge that nought but death shall ever deprive me."

" Hush !" interrupted Emeline, " footsteps disturb the silence---adieu-- to-morrow---let us live upon the hope that we may meet again."

The youth knelt at her feet, pressing her hand to his lips with an in-grafting will.---She withdrew it hastily, but reluctantly, and was on the point of quitting the grotto, when her farther progress was stopped by Sir Launcelot and Uberto ; who, drawn to the spot by the sounds of their voices, rushed in, and seized upon their persons."

This sudden, and unexpected interruption, took the young lovers, as it were, by storm ; a cloud of sorrow was cast over all their previous happiness---their fondest wishes had received a check, and neither of them could utter a syllable. At length Sir Launcelot broke the silence by de-manding the reason of his daughter's lengthened disappearance from among the company.

Emeline, replied not, and her father gazed wildly on Calthart---against whom he had become greatly incensed within the last few moments, through a conversation he had held with the wily Uberto, relating to the young knight.     He had also seized upon him with so firm a grasp, that every attempt, made upon the part of Calthart to disengage himself, was utterly unsuccessful.    In the mean while, the robber held the fainting body of the maiden in his arms, and stood by the side of the knight, closely watching a chance to escape with his burthen unperceived.

The moon now became darkened by a thick black cloud passing over her surface, and, for a time, the whole party became invisible to each other.

"Ha! ha!—mine—mine!" cried the pretended abbot, as, seizing Emeline in his arms, he dashed onward towards the forest, leaving the enraged knights to settle matters how they best could.

In a very short time he was on the drawbridge; he had no time to give the signal, and was, therefore rather awkwardly placed.    None could he see around---all was still, and silent as the grave.    Taking, therefore, a path known but to himself, Uberto hastened on with his burthen.

---

## CHAP. V.

### THE STRANGER'S SECOND ESSAY TO BEFRIEND EMELINE.

Uberto rushed hastly on with his captive; at length, however, he was alarmed by the sound of horses hoofs from behind.    Stopping to listen more attentively, he soon discovered it was but a single horseman.    Fearless of any single individual, whether friend or foe, Uberto coolly resumed his journey.    His unknown follower quickly overtook him.    It was the tall stranger who had rescued Emeline from the power of Hugh Cuthlin.

"Stop, knave!" cried he, in a voice of thunder.

Uberto stopped.    "What would'st thou with me, sir stranger?" said he, calmly, not wishing to appear at all surprised, or why dost thou disturb a peaceable traveller in this dark wood?"

"Traveller! thou night owl," sneered the stranger; "but hark ye, knave—if thou hast a sword, defend thyself."

The next moment two glittering blades quivered in the moon beams. A contest, which would certainly have ended in the death of one or other of the combatants, was hardly begun, ere a dozen stout fellows, led on by Freeman, rushed to the spot.

"Who is this, your enemy?" cried Freeman.

"Ah, *who?*" echoed the chieftian; "but no matter, his hardihood shall meet its due reward."

"It shall," chuckled Freeman, drawing his hand significantly across his throat.    "But why didst thou neglect the proposed signal of the light?"

"I cannot now explain," said Uberto, hastily; "fly with the damsel to our retreat—she will then be beyond the power of our enemies."

"And the reach of her friends," rejoined Freeman, who immediately placed the swooning maid across his horse's saddle and took his departure.

"Gag the prisoner, and drag him to the cave;" said Uberto to the remaining members of his death-dealing band.

*(To be continued.)*

# GARDEN OF ROMANCE.

## FANNY GREENWELL;
### OR,
### THE OLD FARM HOUSE.
*[Continued from our last.]*

He now tore open the letter, scanning its contents with violent and trembling emotion; at last, overpowered by his feelings, he sunk into a chair, and, dropping the letter, covered his eyes with his hands.

"Good Heaven! Mr. Greenwell," cried George, "wherefore this emotion?"

The farmer replied only by pointing to the letter, which George picked up.

"My own dear Fanny," said George, reading, "signed 'Melville.' The libertine!"

The sounds of music and laughter from the joyous throng without now rung in the ears of the farmer, and presently two or three of the rustics entered with the barrel of ale.

"Stop, stop I say," shouted Greenwell, "the voice of melody, near misery's dwelling, is mockery to nature."

"Father, dear father, why do you speak so harshly?" cried Sophy, who had entered with the rustics; "what is it moves you thus?"

"That which would move a flint!" shrieked Greenwell. "My happy home, my little cottage of content, thy peace, thy charm has fled for ever; it is childish to see an old man weep, but these are not tears of sorrow, but of anger, deep and rooted anger. Where is she? Tell me. Swift as the lightning be your speech! Where is she?"

"Whom—Fanny?"

"Aye, *Fanny!*" echoed Greenwell bitterly, "the—the object of all my care, the only being on the earth that ever planted in my heart a fear—where is she?"

No. 5.

" She was here but now, and will return speedily ; she said as much."

" Then she told thee falsely ; she will return no more !" cried Michael Wright, who had just entered.

" No more !" echoed all.

" No, I am sorry to say—"

" Out with it man ; why dost thou falter in thy tale ? what stays thy speech ? there are none here but her own blood, her own friends ; what art sorry for ?"

" Fanny has fled to London with Squire Melville," said Michael.

" Pursue ! pursue !" cried several.

" 'Tis useless," retorted Michael, " the chaise flew like the wind !"

" Stir not a step—let her go, base, vile ingrate as she is," cried Greenwell. " Heart hold firm, burst not yet—the wayward, thoughtless child ; emblem of innocence, as I thought her ; and she was innocent as the light of Heaven 'till that villain poisoned her pure mind, dazzled her weak sight ! But my revenge is yet to come ; I'll have it—I'll have it ere I die ! I'll hunt him o'er the limits of the earth ! Stir not a step, breathe not a sound to stay her ! let her go, and with her—"

" Ah ! do not—do not curse her !" screamed Sophy, seizing the uplifted arms of her father, and holding them down.

The farmer now staggered to a chair, and insensibility happily put a short period to his bitter anguish.

---

## CHAP. V.

THE SQUIRE'S TOWN HOUSE.—LOVE IN HUMBLE LIFE.—THERE'S NOBODY BY, YOU MAY TAKE A BUSS.

Seven years—seven long, long years must now be considered as passed, since the enactment of the striking incidents of our last chapter, and the flight of Fanny, from her girlhood's home—" Home !" some one has said " the word is magical to an English ear, conjuring up ' bright images of rest ' —fireside evenings when the snow lies on the ground ; mirth from the heart, and without alloy ; sacred ties binding hearts to hearts ; freedom and a sanctuary from the follies and malevolence of the earth. What woman born in beloved England loves not home ? Her most precious privileges are enshrined in that ark of gold. There is her sphere of greatness ; to reform, to regulate, to purify, to exalt, to refine, to exert her utmost energies, to endure with the sublimest piety. Home is her temple ; and nowhere can she better hallow her God, or work out his precepts than there."

Notwithstanding all these sacred ties—to which we might add many others, if possible still more sacred, Fanny quitted her father's roof, and, proceeding to Melville Hall, the pledge of matrimony (whether real or not remains to be seen) was immediately administered to her and the young Squire Vincent Melville, by a clerical friend of his, named Mortimer ; after which they started direct for the Squire's splendid town residence in Grosvenor Square ; and in which place they have now resided, in a state of sumptuous elegance, for seven years. We must here, however, make a slight digression.

Becky Wibbles, being at length tired of tormenting Mat Maythorn, went to London, where she succeeded in engaging herself to Mrs. Melville, in whose service Jemmy Jenkins, her more favored lover, had been for some time. Becky soon found means to confront Jemmy, whom she found to have become very foppish, speaking affectedly, and with a strong lisp; and accosted him thus—

"He, he, he, Jemmy!"

"Jemmy! how *ri*-diculous that sounds, Miss *Re*-becca! don't say Jemmy! in the squares, they call me Mr. James—Mr. James, call me Miss *Re*-becca."

"Oh, come, none o' thee nonsense, Jemmy—I ax pardon, but thee winna be offended, Mr. James. Dost remember the day thou wast breeched? I does—mother let me paper my hair that very day! Gracious o' marey there be no pleasurement in thee eyes lad, but wi' old acquaintances, the will for the deed a' the world over!"

Jemmy tried to smile, and affectedly took a pinch of snuff.

"Ah, that be right lad," said Becky

"Lad!" echoed Jemmy; "horseshoes and assafœtida! What *ruling* star predominated to bring this little *creeter* to the *realms* of the gay!"

"Whatever beest thee chattering about Jemmy?—Mr. James I mean. Drat it, who ha' soaped thee scull, Jemmy. I didn't observe it afore!"

These enquiries so affected Jemmy, that he fell back into a chair.

"Here you sarving girls, have you any brown paper, or a bottle o' vinegar? The lad be bad!" cried Becky. "Jemmy—I mean Mr. Jan. ; be sick—burnt paper or a drop of brandy!"

"Burnt paper! Ugh, ugh! Eau de Cologne," said Jemmy, shuddering at the bare idea of such vulgar restoratives.

"Cologne! who's he?" asked Becky.

"I must *resign*—I can't stand this—I'll tell her so," growled Jemmy, rising. "Miss *Re*-becca!" he cried.

"Come, none o' thee flummery," replied she; "thee used to call I Beck or Becky arter a hard day's plough or harrowing. Jemmy, what ha' thee done wi' the highlows uncle made for thee?"

"Highlows! I'm sinking, and I can't suppress it!" exclaimed Jemmy, again having recourse to the snuff-box.

"Don't be poking that filthy stuff up thee nose," cried Becky, knocking the box from his hand, "you aint parson o' parish at home; by and bye I'll see thee taking it wi' a spoon from thy waistcoat pocket."

Jemmy literally gazed at her with astonishment.

"Solid silver, as I'm a vargin," muttered Becky, picking it up again. Once more restoring it to her companion, she said—"Jemmy, what a queer chap you be! long ago, in our own village, you used to say, ' Becky, beautiful Beck, gi' us a buss, lass!' and thee'd not ask, but take it. I—I'd kiss thee for old 'quaintance, Jemmy," she added, wiping her lips.

"'Quaintance!" echoed Jemmy; "roses and lilies for the remembrance of green fields. I'll taste the nectar of thy *ruby* lips, Miss *Re*-becca."

"None o' the fooling."

"Becky, Beck—"

" Ah! I knows my name, and I aint impudent," returned Becky; "there's nobody by, you may take a buss!"

Jemmy having availed himself of Becky's offer, she resumed—

" Come now, sit thee down, lad, and I'll tell'ee all about it! Squire Melville—bless his old heart—told I, if I wished to come to London, I should have a sarvice wi' his son, and I ha' got it. Jemmy! Jemmy, dear Jemmy! the poor girl's heart ha' found a resting place—it is here, wi' her first, her only love!"

" What would Miss *Rachel Roberts*, my lady's maid, say to this?" thought Jemmy, who replied—

" Miss *Rebecca*, that is, I mean Becky Wibbles, you see—at least, I do—there is a *respectable* lady, one Miss *Rachel Roberts*, to whom I have paid my devoirs, and although the limitude of a gentleman's gentleman's means would not permit a special licence, we have adopted the *re*gular course of being united by banns."

" I—I don't understand—yes, oh yes I—I do!" cried Becky; "you're a deceiver—I aint unpacked my boxes yet, nor will I! I—I 'ont live here. They told me at home I should be happy, but I sha'nt, for I've lost my lad's love. I arn't ashamed to own it, for that that is honest has no fear—Mat Maythorn said as much!"

" Mat Maythorn! the *ruffian*!" drawled Jemmy.

" No Jemmy—Mat is simple, but he's an honest man! he said soft things to a young lass, but she gave no heed to them. Good bye—I'll go home again, I'll never breathe a word but where 'tis welcome. Gi' me the green fields, and the heart that is honest. Let me tell you, Jemmy—*Mister* James, I mean—I've thirteen and fourpence yet,—there's the waggon, sir—though it goes slowly, it comes at last to an end—and in that end there's a husband! I 'ont even say good-bye, you deceiver, you—you—you—Banns! Miss Rachel Roberts, indeed! when you hear again of me I'm Mrs. Mathew Maythorn! I'm a weak woman, but I'm a desperate one!—only I've left my pattens down stairs, I could knock you on the head, so I could, Mister Jemmy."

Thus giving vent to her spleen, Becky rushed passionately from the room.

" 'Pon my veracity, but the gal has spirit," drawled Jemmy. " I'm in extatics! *Really* I didn't reckon the *transfer* of Mr. James Jenkin's love and *regard* would have passed off so well! A *rustic* like that, who is as *rusty* as a hosses shoe over a barn door, to aspire to me, is *remarkably rediculous* in the extreme! Now, lovely *Rachel Roberts*, I'm all your own."

" You see I hanna gone yet, Mr. Jemmy," shouted Becky, re-entering the apartment. " I be come back to tell 'ee a bit of my mind."

" Miss *Re*-becca, don't dist*ress* yourself," sneered Jemmy, dusting the handsome covered chairs with his pocket handkerchief.

" Distress myself! What about thee, thee ugly toad? Not I. Dost know what this is?" she continued, at the same time holding forth the valentine at which Mat Maythorn had been so much annoyed.

" Yes," answered Jemmy, " a thingamy—a—a—a—"

" No it beant a thingamerry, nor a ha—ha—ha—" cried Becky, grinding out the words from between her teeth; " It's a *wallingtine*, from

( *To be continued.*)

# EMELINE;
## CR,
# THE LOVE PLEDGE.

[*Continued from page* 32.]

" The knave has contrived to give us the slip," cried one.

" S'death !" vociferated the chieftain furiously, " why did ye let the villain escape ? he may throw the pursuers on our track—away with ye all, to the cave—away I say, quick !"

Another moment, Uberto alone remained ; he had taught his band obedience, and they had never forgotten the lesson.

" This will never do," he muttered as he quitted the spot and made his way through the fern and high grass, " I must cast off my disguise and keep well on the alert, or all will not proceed as I wish. Poor Sir Launcelot," he continued " to take me for the Abbot Rainsford—I should think his zeal for the Holy Church will be rather cooled ; by the mass, mine would —ha, ha !"

" Ha, ha !" echoed a shrill voice, in a tone of derision.

" Marry, but that's marvellous," muttered the robber, peering wistfully through a clump of trees.

All was, however, silent, and nothing—save the soft sighings of the western breeze as it swept lightly along the expanded boughs of the forest trees, which were gilded with a flood of silver light—disturbed the impressive solitude of the scene.

Thinking it useless to loiter about in idle speculation, Uberto disengaged himself of his monkish robes, and, secreting them in the hollow of an old tree, looked once more enquiringly around him, and then bent his steps toward the castle ruins, which the robbers had cognomised as the " Owlet's Haunt."

## CHAP. V.

### A LOVERS RESOLVE—THE PURSUIT.

The struggles of Sir Launcelot and Calthart were at length brought to a close, by a shrill voice loudly exclaiming.—

" Sir Launcelot !—fly to the aid of thy daughter—see ye not she is gone from thee ? to the forest, quick—it may not yet be too late ; but delay not as ye value her safety—away, I say—away !"

The old man gazed hurriedly around him—Emeline was indeed gone, and leaving his imaginary enemy unharmed, he rushed precipitately from the bower.

Calthart proceeded dejectedly to the hall. Here every thing wss altered from its former gay appearance—all was bustle and confusion, and amidst the tumult he heard Sir Launcelot shouting to his domestics to arm, and accompany him in quest of his daughter ; but without awaiting their attendance he darted off at full speed towards the forest.

The young lover seemed at a loss how to act. His eyes protruded from their sockets—his lip quivered—his countenance was ashy pale ; in fact, all, all but too plainly revealed the bitter intensity of his mental agony.

At length he made an effort to shake off his oppressive weakness, and began in good earnest to take immediate steps for the maiden's restoration.

" Sir Knights," he exclaimed, " are ye willing to join me in an enter-prize of great moment ?"

" Of what nature ?" was the rejoinder.

" There was one among the festivities habited in the garb of a monk."

" There was, the Abbot Rainsford !"

" Well, then," continued Calthart this *Abbot Rainsford,* as he styles himself, is none other than Uberto the Robber King !"

" Indeed !"

" Aye, *indeed* !—he is now bold enough to approach our dwellings, nay, unblushingly bear off those we most prize."

" Is he thus courageous ?" cried one.

" He is," said Calthart; " the beauteous Emeline is even now in his power—I would wrest her from the ruffian, say will ye aid me with your blades ?"

The knights hesitated.   They knew, by bitter experience, Uberto would be fully prepared to meet them. The proposer, however, was not to be daunted by anything save a decided refusal; this they of course could not give, and Calthart again ardently exclaimed.

" Knights of the Cross, honored by the appellative of " brave," will you pursue this lawless destroyer of our peace, or resign the title of knights for ever ?"

The effect of his address was instantaneous—each hand grasped a sword-hilt, and with one voice they expressed their determination to follow, rescue or perish in the attempt.

They quickly proceeded to the court-yard, where the steeds awaited their various owners.

" Your steeds, like myself, are anxious to depart," said Calthart; " mount and draw up in a line, we can then arrange matters satisfactory to all."

The mandate was obeyed, the line formed, and, as our hero rode slowly down the rank, he ascertained the number of his brave followers amounted to thirty-five.

" Now," said he, " appoint a leader and let us away."

" We submit to your guidance," cried several.

" 'Tis well ; but we had better divide our band into two companies. You, Sir Gilbert St. Clare, will please to take fifteen from our number, and pursue the more direct road leading north of the forest; miss not a place—let not a single spot in your rout remain untraced.   Having so done, if unsuccessful, meet me at the eastern part of the old castle ruins ; but mark me—should you meet our hated enemies, blow a shrill blast—that shall be the signal."

" It shall !"

" And at the Almanza ruins we meet ?"

" We do."

The gallant bands dashed onward over the green carpet of the forest, sword-in-hand, for each soul was bent on terribly avenging the insult of-fered the ' presiding genius ' of their late happy carousal.   Onward they rode speeding with giant strides over glade and glen ; one was past, ano-ther, and another hill was ascended and descended—rivers were crossed, ditches were leaped, and like as in our modern steeple-chases, nothing was an obstacle, nothing retarded their progress, for on—on they went.

## CHAP. VI.

"A greater pow'r than we can contradict
Hath thwarted our intents."—SHAKSPEARE.

### SHOWETH THAT CUNNING OFT RISES SUPERIOR TO BRAVERY.

According to his leader's command, Freeman, at the top of his speed, bore his charge in the direction of the ruins. His steed was a matchless creature, nor was its burthen sufficiently weighty to retard its swift career. As the robber neared the ivy-mantled remains of the old castle, he rather slackened his rein to gaze on the form of his prisoner. Raising her delicate face toward him, and gently removing her luxuriant auburn tressess from her brow, he was struck with admiration of her superlative beauty. He now heard the trampling of horses feet, and being remarkable for coolness and great discernment, he exercised the latter quality by immediately urging his steed behind a grove of trees. He was not much before-hand in his movement. In a very short time up came the party he had heard but a littlg time before, and halted directly opposite the spot he had chosen for a place of concealment. They were well mounted, and, to his surprise, commanded by Sir Calthart Burgoyne, whom he instantly recognised.

The outlaw patted the neck of his well-tutored animal with great kindness; the beautiful creature stood death-like still, and he listened attentively to the converse of his pursuers.

"This is the road pointed out by the mysterious stranger we lately encountered, is it not?" said Calthart.

"It is."

"Then they must be well horsed, at any rate."

"They must!"

Whether or not the voices of her friends acted lik a charm on Freeman's hitherto fainting companion we cannot venture to opine, but she at this moment revived, and, opening her fine blue eyes, gazed full on his swarthy countenance. The robber felt himself awkwardly situated;—softly did he whisper for her to be calm—gently did he raise her on his saddle—mild and kindly did he smile to hush her mind to peace. This might have succeeded in its object, had not the voice of Calthart fell suddenly on her ear, when her situation burst on her mind in all its horrors. Giving one loud scream for help, she again swooned away in the arms of Freeman.

A moment had scarce passed ere a dozen swords were pointed at his breast, and the bridle of his horse was roughly seized.

"Villian!" vociferated Calthart, "surrender, or I will command thy instant death, quick! or every sword here finds it's way to your heart!"

"Pshaw! for whom dost thou take me, that thou seekest to intimidate me with thy paltry threats?" cried Freeman; "meet me singly and prove your vaunted courage!"

Calthart raised his sword, the bright blade glittered in the moonbeams, and would have quickly descended on the head of Freeman had he not hastily drew his dirk from his belt, and raising it high in the air, loudly exclaimed—

"Beware!—the first sword that falls, seals my captive's death warrant!"

"Villain!" cried Calthart, "your life is at present safe, but from this spot you stir not without resiguing the innocent object of your malice."

This was like a vision of hope to Freeman, who at once determined to make an effort to escape. Backing his steed a few paces, the robber prepared to make a sudden spring over the opposing rank.

Calthart perceiving his manœuvre, caused his companions to form two lines, one a short distance in the rear of the other. This was an ill-directed movement. The robber saw that he was no longer surrounded, and once more patting the neck of his horse, the noble animal, snuffing the air, dashed off in an opposite direction, at a pace which defied the chances of being again overtaken. Gaily did the beautiful creature fly over the ground—gaily did her hoofs transport her rider over hillock and glade; at length he slackened his pace, and proceeded onward like one without the reach of danger, which indeed he now was, as will shortly be seen.

" We are defeated this time, at all events," cried Calthart, after a sharp ride, " for see you not yon figure of an horseman bearing something in his arms ? How leisurely he seems to ride up the castle hill."

It was Freeman.

" By St. Mary he deserves credit for an horseman, as much as he merits the gallows-tree for a rogue" he continued ; " however, we will now seek Gilbert. The convent of St. Fredrica stands but a mile or two hence whither we will then proceed."

Dost thou mean to resign the chase then ?" cried one.

" For a short time, I do," said Calthart; " you see the day begins to break, and they will be able to watch our movements too easily.

A dusky veil by which the earth had been enveloped for the last few moments now gradually ascended, and the east was soon after enrobed with clouds of beautiful blue, tinged here and there with streaks of crimson and sparkling gold.

" We can do nothing more till night again shields us by its ebon mantle" said Calthart, " I will then borrow a lute, staff, and Rosary, of the good Abbot of St Fredrica, and, personating a wandering minstrel, reconnoitre the robbers stronghold. Under a plea of want I may gain admittance, I can then easily ascertain in what part of the castle Emeline is secreted, and by that means render an attack easy and effectual. Be you near the northern entrance, and when my plot is ripe I will whistle three times—rush across the portcullis, cutting down all that dare dispute your progress, and we may this night, exterminate the whole band !"

The gallant troop once more resumed their journey, little recking that the whole of their important designs had been overheard. Such, however, was the fact. The sound of their voices had attracted the attention of one of the robbers, named Caspero, as he was prowling about the forest in search of plunder, who, secreting himself behind a clump of trees, listened breathlessly to every word they uttered.

## CHAP, VII

### THE CONVENT—THE SICK CHAMBER—AN UNEXPECTED RESULT.

They were soon joined by Sir Gilbert St. Clair, whom Calthart informed of his intention of visiting the robbers' cave in the garb of a minstrel.

"The enterprise will be attended by considerable danger," said Sir Gilbert.

*(To be continued.)*

# PENNY ILLUSTRATED

# GARDEN OF ROMANCE.

## FANNY GREENWELL;

### OR,

### THE OLD FARM HOUSE.

**Mr. Jemmy Jenkins in Lunnun to Becky Wibbles in the country.**—I come back to gi' it thee, and likewise to tell 'ee not to be 'dressing any more o' thee rubbish to Becky Wibbles, for Becky Wibbles 'ont be Becky Wibbles any more than three weeks, and a day or so, for I'll make Mat go to clerk and publish banns afore I sit down at home; and if ever thee comes wi' young Squire down to our parts, doant 'ee be chatting any o' thee flummery, or squeezing my hand as thee used to do, or thee'lt stand a good chance o' getting thee jacket warmed by Mat's whip. Oh, I doant want anything to remind me o' thee, thee viper," cried she, hurling the valentine towards him—"there's thee *wallingtine*, send it to Miss Rachel Roberts —he,—he—he!"

So saying she again flounced out of the room and hurried to the kitchen. Seizing her box (which still remained unpacked) with giant-like strength, she rushed out of the house, and, proceeding rapidly to the waggon office, paid her passage back to the country.

"What a fortunate escape," cried Jemmy, as soon as he was alone. "I'd a great mind to have made her a splendid offer of protection, and a garret in the neighborhood of our square, but I'm glad I didn't! Dem it, James, you're a martyr to morality, you prodigal, you are!"

### CHAP. VI.

**ALL IS NOT GOLD THAT GLITTERS—THE VISIT—RETROSPECTION—
A SURPRISE—FATE OF THE SQUIRE.**

"The or-molu dial has chimed two," ejaculated Fanny, who was lounging on a superb couch. " I'm getting a very sluggard, have varied nature, and turned the night to day, yet my heart wearies at these busy scenes the world mis-term gay and joyous; my boy—my darling boy is now my only source of happiness—when he is not with me, I linger for the village green with its glassy streamlet, and the sunlit fields of golden grain; and the happy, smiling faces who were partners of my childhood's sports. But—but these are joys long—long since passed away, never to return. Let me banish such thoughts for ever from my mind, they are unfitting the—the wife of Vincent Melville!"

The door of the apartment was now opened by Jemmy Jenkins, who, entering, said—

" Pardon me, my lady, for this intrusion, but there is a man below who rejects all refusal. I told him master was from home, and he expresses a wish for an interview with your ladyship!"

" Is he a nameless man?" asked Fanny. " Who is he? and whence comes he?"

" He says his name is Michael Wright, and he comes from Melville Hall."

" Show him up!"

" Here, my lady?"

" Yes, here! and without a moment's loss of time!"

" Most assuredly, my lady!" said Jemmy, who, leaving the apartment, muttered—

" When will she rub off the rust of her rustic ideas?"

" And Michael Wright has come to the gay city!" soliloquised Fanny. " What associations come with the name of Michael Wright!—My village swain—my ruddy Adonis in the summer stroll—my—my companion—my shy companion by the winter's fire in the dear old farm house!"

Her train of thought was here interrupted by the re-appearance of Jenkins, who, preceding Michael, ushered him into her presence, making, as he did so, several low bows. Michael Wright could not refrain from bursting into a loud laugh at the affected manner of his old playmate who pretended not to recognise him, but upon seeing Mrs. Melville his merriment was at an end.

" The precious lout!" growled the offended Jemmy, as he retired, " I —I should like to—to tumble him into the mill-stream!"

" Then why don't you?" cried one of the other servants, to whom Jemmy had related the supposed insult.

" I can't!" said Jemmy.

" Why can't you?" enquired the other.

" I—I—that is—he—he wouldn't let me," said Jemmy, which caused the whole of the servants to laugh long and loud. But to our tale—

" What, Michael! and how dost do, Michael?" enquired Fanny.

" Oh, I'm lovely, thank'ee; hope you be the same?" returned Michael. " Why I be shot if I hardly know thee, decked out in these fal lals. Lord, lord, they be mortal smart, surely, but how deadly pale thee dost look; there be roses twisted in thy tresses, but Lunnun smoke ha' killed the prettiest one—the one that used to bloom on thy cheek!"

Fanny uttered a deep sigh.

" Why don't thee smile as thee used to do at home?" continued Michael.

" Lord, I—I be so overjoyed to see thee I could almost cry !—Gi's thee hand, lass—I—I ax pardon—Miss—Missus—Madam, I mean."

" There Michael !" said Fanny, extending her hand, " 'tis the grasp of your old friend ; from my heart I'm glad to see you, Michael. Come, sit down, and we'll talk of old times and of old friends, and—and the dear farm house."

" Oh, bless those blue eyes of yours—I—I—There's a heart throbbing here at the mention of your words, for they wake up memory of times that be gone and past, and the heart must be as still as death can make it ere it can forget. Thee thinkest sometimes, then, of the old stile, the beech grove, and the—Oh, Madam you make me a child again !" and he dashed away the tears that were fast gathering in his eyes.

" I do—I do," sighed Fanny. " Oh, blessed be days of our childhood, for they were of innocence—without guile—without care. Ours was the realm of a fairy land, and Happiness was king. Come, then, playmate of my young days—my girlhood's beau—the boy who strove to win a girl's love,—tell me of those scenes of our walks in the beautiful glade, on the summer's nights ; 'twas then, when the heavens above were spangled with myriads of glittering gems—'twas then—a—a maiden heard your tale of love, aye, and *heeded* it, Michael ! but Time is a mighty master, and works many changes—Melville came and Michael—"

" Poor Michael was forgotten !"

" Not so ! he was always regarded as a friend, as a brother ! I'm in the green fields again, where the fresh air breathed heavenly pure,—it was a joy I ne'er can hope to taste here in this peopled city. Come Michael, be quick, tell me of my father, my—my stern father ! I can almost— seeing you—fancy him before me,—tell me of Sophy—of the old man— of—of the dear old farm house !"

" Why, there be tears in your beautiful eyes," said Michael, " pray dry them, do'ee ; I never saw thee weep till now,—thee feyther be well !"

" Bless you," cried Fanny, " Heaven's blessing be on him and you ! Oh, how I have longed to hear those words. I have written oft to him, but I have angered, disobeyed, aye, deceived him ! I was a fool to—to expect forgiveness, for though I fled my home, on many a sleepless night my thought, my heart was resting there. But how is Sophy ? Is she well ? Is she happy ?"

" Well, and happy as the day is long !" said Michael.

" That her day of joy may never know an end," sobbed Fanny, " is her sister's earnest prayer. Now of thyself, Michael ; art wedded yet ?"

" No, I'm thinking I be cut out for an old bachelor,—I an't courageous enough to say soft things to lasses," replied Michael.

" There was a time when you might have won a wife, but for your boyish shyness. You had no rival *then*, Michael. You told one tale, and told no more ; *he* came and—. But we will not talk of that. What is it brings thee up to town ?"

" Old Squire Melville be ill, a' most dying !" said Michael.

" Heaven avert that calamity," ejaculated Fanny ; " it would make my husband wretched."

" Husband !" echoed Michael unconsciously.

" Michael Wright, why do you echo that word ?" cried Fanny. " Is he not my husband?   Lives there a breath to throw a blight against that holy tie?   Why fall your eyes to the earth, Michael?   Speak, has scandal fell upon the name of one you call your earliest friend?   Hast thou lost thy power of speech, Michael?   Speak! there is a meaning in your silence.—A terror in your looks!  Speak! speak!. or I shall sink at your feet.  Speak—speak."

"Well, if I must," returned Michael, "They do say young squire 'ticed thee from thee home to the hall,—that his friend Mortimer, who were once a minister, had been stripped of his gown, and the ceremony be not binding."

Fanny was so much overcome by this unexpected intelligence that she sunk back in her chair as though she were paralysed.

"Don't, don't take on so," faltered Michael—"I and many others believe they belied you?"

"Bless you, for so much charity," sobbed Fanny.   "Oh, it was bravely done to stab a weak woman's fame, and no voice near her to tell the tale—to—to breathe the poisonous words, which, when they fall upon the ear, must penetrate to the heart, and bow it down to rise no more.   But there is a mighty prop whose name is Truth to hold it firm, guileless, and unsullied.   I hear Melville approaching—you shall hear it from his lips,—you shall hear him swear, in the face of Heaven, even in thought they've wronged me.   Retire but for a moment.   I wonder not now,' she continued, as she ushered Michael into an ante-room and closed the door upon him, " oh, no, I wonder not now at my father's, sister's silence—it was not natural they could own a blackened wretch as they supposed me to be ; but Michael shall hear him call upon God to witness he has done me no wrong, he shall—he shall !"

At this moment Vincent Melville rushed into the chamber as though he had been hunted by bloodhounds.

"Melville!   Vincent!   What means this haste?"  cried Fanny, in alarm ; "that frenzied look of horror, what does it portend,—tell—tell me —quick Vincent, quick."

"There—there is scarcely time !"  shrieked the Squire, licking his parched lips, which appeared completely bloodless—"there—there is death and danger in—in this delay !"

"Tell me—pray tell me what has occurred?"  urged Fanny.

"My—my prodigality has proved my bane," roared Melville, his eyes nearly starting from their sockets, "it—it has stripped our boy of his inheritance, it has robbed his father of his—his fair name ; the world will soon know him as the beggared child of one who—who beggared many !"

"What madness is this?   What is it you mean?"  said Fanny.

"That—that reckless extravagance has—has led to crime !"

A loud noise of hasty footsteps were now heard rapidly approaching the chamber in which they were conversing.

"They come—they come !" roared the Squire ; " there is not a moment left—the law agents are on my footsteps—hide me—hide me—save me from ignominy—from—from death !   They are at the door.   'Tis flight alone can save me !"

So saying Vincent Melville rushed precipitately into the same apartment in which was Michael Wright, and strongly fastened it from within.

"Has then the bolt of misery fallen on us all?" sobbed Fanny. "Crime !
(*To be continued.*)

# EMELINE;
### OR,
## THE LOVE PLEDGE.

"It may be," returned Calthart; "but I always hope for the best, and defy the worst, by which means I overcome many a difficulty."

"Your acts, like the castle built on a rock, are founded with judgment," said the other, "for certainly the man who ever anticipates imaginary dangers, is never prepared to withstand the shock of real ones."

Calthart smiled. "I fear Sir Gilbert, you are becoming a parasite," said he.

"On my soul, no," returned Sir Gilbert, warmly; "to prove the sincerity of my words, I will join thee in thy perilous undertaking."

"Be it so then; now my brave companions, we must away—follow me."

The newly-risen sun streamed in among the branches of the fresh green trees—the uncultured flowerets of the forest were bespangled with dewy moisture—and the note of the lark sounded shrill and beautiful in the ears of our adventurers as they proceeded towards the convent of St. Fredrica. At length they arrived thither, and Sir Calthart applied his hand to the bell. The summons was quickly answered by the Abbot Francesco, from the tower, and our hero craved admission. The Abbot, casting a keen glance at the enquirer, demanded his name. The reply, whatever it might be, was evidently a satisfactory one, a moment having scarce past ere the massy gate creaked on its time-worn hinges, and the whole party made their *entree*. Francesco conducted all but Calthart to the refectory ; our hero, however, with whom the Abbot seemed to be well acquainted, he ushered to his own private apartment, and placing some refreshments before him, he said—

" Having to visit a wounded gentleman, who has but lately become an inmate of the priory, I must now leave thee ; do thou, however, enjoy thyself till my return."

The Abbot was about to quit the apartment, when Calthart exclaimed, " May not I accompany thee ?"

" If such is thy wish, follow !" said Francesco ; who quickly conducted him to the chamber where lay the wounded stranger. The window blinds were closely drawn, which cast an air of gloom on the surrounding objects. A small lighted lamp stood on an antique table of black polished oak, shedding a sickly gleam a short space around, but rendering distant objects undefinable. Francesco silently approached the bedside, and kindly enquired if the object of his hospitality felt better. 'A little,' was the faint rejoinder. Calthart heard the reply. The voice though suppressed to a whisper seemed familiar to him, and he rushed up to the bedside.

" Good God !" he exclaimed, taking the stranger's hand, " 'tis Sir Launcelot Shadwell !"

The knight raised his head, a faint smile of recognition played o'er his pale features, and he again sunk back on the pillow in a state of exhaustion.

" Is this unfortunate gent thy friend ?" asked Francesco, in a tone of surprise.

" He is !" pr'y thee attend him zealously, and thou shalt be richly rewarded."

" The pleasure arising from the performance of a good act, is a guerdon richer far than man has the power to award," said the abbot, warmly.

" That is a noble sentiment," rejoined Calthart—" a sentiment well worthy of him whom I am assured can fully feel the bitter intensity of another's earthly trials, and spareth no pains to alleviate them."

However pleasing to the abbot these enconiums might have been, or whether administering comfort to the distressed was by him considered merely an act of duty embodying the beautiful precept of " brotherly love," and, consequently, unworthy such warmth of praise as Calthart had bestowed, we know not ; though certain it is, he wished to turn the conversation into another channel, for which purpose he rang a small bell, and two attendants entered.

" Attend the wants of our sick guest till my return," said the abbot.

" The two men, who were monks, immediately seated themselves by the bed-side, and Francesco beckoned Sir Calthart Burgoyne from the room.

" Thou hadst better seek a little repose, sir knight," said he ; 'twill prove a sweet solace after the extreme fatigue thou hast endured. I must court my morning devotions, but I will again see thee a few hours hence."

They had by this time reached the apartment the abbot had kindly appropriated to the use of Calthart, and, pronouncing a blessing, he bade him adieu.

The busy scene in which our hero had been so prominent an actor had hitherto given him but little time for reflection ; now, however, he was alone, and the stirring events of the preceding night rushed upon his mind with amazing rapidity. Again was he engaged in fierce warfare with

Hugh Cuthlin (who had since died from a fatal wound administered by the strange pursuer of Uberto in defence of Emeline)—again was he shouting for Freeman to resign his charge—and again did he behold the ruffian's shining dagger as it gleamed above the fair one's head. Now would his thoughts revert to the sad fate of Sir Launcelot, who, in searching for his daughter, had met two of the robbers, and seizing one of them tightly by the throat, could only be repulsed by the dagger's point. This event made him resolve to lose no time in seeking to obtain a more speedy revenge, and that he would visit the Almanza ruins as soon as he could possibly procure the necessary disguise. Slumber, sweet and refreshing slumber, at length dissolved his agony of mind, and 'balmy dreams' assumed an elfin revelry over the heart but lately racked with unquenchable and bitter grief. After the lapse of a few hours he arose, and seeking the worthy abbot enquired for the minstrels' garbs for himself and friend.

"Thou shalt have them, my son, and may God shield thee in the righteousness of thy cause," said Francesco, rising to unlock an iron chest. "Here are the vestments," he added, producing them, "who is thy fellow?"

"Gilbert St. Clair."

Sir Gilbert was immediately summoned. They were soon arrayed, and the abbot conducted them to the gate, where they were met by their companions. A smile of satisfaction ran through the assembly as they beheld the metamorphosis, which was only checked by the idea of a discovery, though such an event seemed hardly possible. Taking each proffered hand, and shaking it warmly, the knights knelt to receive the abbot's farewell blessing, and taking their leave, soon lost sight of that holy place, which had proved so welcome a sanctuary in the hour of need. The sun had gained its meridian, but its intense heat was softened by an invigorating breeze, and our adventurers continued their journey with all possible expedition. At length they reached the castle. The drawbridge was down, but guarded by one of the lawless band, who, astonished at the sight of strangers so near their haunt, gruffly demanded their business.

"'Tis with your lordly master," said Calthart, with well feigned ignorance of the character of the man he was addressing.

"My master is no lord. And yet he may be, too," muttered the robber. "It strikes me, though, these are the gentry Caspero said would indulge us with a visit—a friendly one, of course—at least, what I consider friendly, that is, to cut as many throats as comes in your way. However, if it prove as I suspect, they play well their parts. Come this way, sir minstrels," he added, shouting the name of Caspero.

"What now?" vociferated Caspero, approaching.

"Here's visitors to our master," cried the other.

"Indeed!" growled Caspero; they'll find good entertainment here, no doubt. Follow me," he added, and they were soon conducted to a neatly-furnished chamber, where, reclining on a couch, and assuming the lofty bearing of a sovereign, was the renowned robber king—Uberto!

A glance explained the chieftain's wish for the absence of his menial, and quitting the apartment, Caspero proceeded to the subterraneous passages that led from the castle to the forest; but remembering he had agreed to meet one of his comrades about that time, he hurriedly returned. Having reached the foot of a flight of steps, he was about to ascend, when a human skeleton, which he saw—or fancied he saw—stayed him in his mad career. He started back with horror—still his eyes were rivetted on this loathsome object. Its arms were extended—its grisly jaws moved—it spoke :—

"WRETCH THY END IS NEAR ! ERE THE SETTING OF ANOTHER SUN, AS I AM, SO WILT THOU BE—BEWARE !"

The dread image of immortality then became invisible, and Caspero rushed from the spot.

## CHAP. VIII.

### THE GRIPE OF DEATH—THE SEVERED HAND—THE HOUR OF RETRIBUTION.

" To what circumstance am I indebted for the unexpected honor of this visit ?" demanded Uberto of his visitors.

" We are poor minstrels," said Calthart, " who humbly crave thy charity."

" Charity ! ha, ha ! thou shalt have it," laughed Uberto, half drawing his sword.

" Whence this unseasonable merriment ?" said Calthart, disconcertedly.

" *Unseasonable !* ho, ho !" cried the robber ; " but no matter, thy dissimulation will prove rather a costly purchase," and he stamped violently on the floor.

Finding themselves thus foiled, Sir Calthart and his noble friend made a simultaneous rush at Uberto with their drawn swords. He was, however, too keen for them—his blade, with which he cut right and left, was drawn in a moment—to all their cuts he found a parry, and with that undaunted coolness a master-hand usually displays, skilfully foiled every effort they made to reach him. The combat was ultimately brought to an end by several of the robbers, who, entering, firmly secured them.

" Drag the knaves to separate dungeons," cried Uberto, dashing the perspiration from his brow.

" At your own peril be it, then," cried Calthart, who, making a sudden spring, burst from his captors ; the next moment one of them lay dead at his feet. The other ruffians seemed rivetted to the spot, so much were they taken by surprise at this unlooked for act of daring and courage. Calthart took advantage of this circumstance, by rushing to a corner, where he stood, sword-in-hand, determinedly awaiting an expected rush upon the part of his enemies.

" Why do ye stand thus unresolved ?" shrieked Uberto ; " on ! I say, or some of ye may share the fate of thy murdered comrade !"

Seeing the position of Calthart, Sir Gilbert thought there was a gleam of hope, and, spurred on still further by an insatiate thirst for vengeance, he curled himself like a snake round the body of one of the robbers, and they both fell heavily to the earth. All eyes were now drawn in this direction, and Calthart's relentless blade was again buried in the heart of another of their enemies.

" Justice will triumph yet !" he cried, as, withdrawing it, the wounded

*(To be continued.)*

# GARDEN OF ROMANCE.

---

## FANNY GREENWELL;

### OR,

### THE OLD FARM HOUSE.

My—my poor desolate boy !—the beggared child of him who—who beggared many ! God of Heaven ! What rushes through my brain !—he —he is a FORGER ?"

" Aye, madam, and our prisoner," cried one of the officers, several of whom had by this time made their *entree*.

Fanny almost sunk to the earth, but making a powerful effort she succeeded in rallying herself.

" Whom—whom is it you seek, gentlemen ?" said she.

" Him of whom you were speaking—Vincent Melville, the forger," cried one.

" You shall not pass to seek him," shrieked Fanny, placing herself, like a second Hercules, before the door of the room he had entered.

" 'Twere needless thinking he can escape," cried one of the officers ; " you may as well banish so foolish a hope—'tis utterly impossible, as the house is surrounded."

" Lost, lost !" cried Fanny, supporting herself by a chair.

A loud wild laugh now rung through the adjacent room, which was immediately followed by the report of that little instrument of death which Byron says

> " Has a strange quick jar upon the ear."

The next moment Michael Wright came forth from his place of concealment, and enquired of whom the officers were in search.

" Vincent Melville ?" cried one ; " he is accused of forgery—he must answer it."

No. 7.

"He *has* answered it !" returned Michael, "he has died by his own hand !"

The dreadful truth of what had occurred now burst, with all its horrors upon the mind of Fanny, who gave utterance to one loud shrill cry, and fell senseless to the earth.

---

## CHAP. VII.

"My heart 'mid all changes. wherever I roam,
Ne'er loses its love for the old house at home."

HOME, SWEET HOME.—THE GIPSIES.—DARK DAVY.—A VILLAIN'S RE-
SOLVE.—ALARM OF FANNY.

As soon as Fanny had sufficiently recovered the shock her mind had sustained from the dreadful intelligence of her husband's crimes, so quickly followed by his untimely end, and had followed him to his last, long, earthly receptacle—the grave ! she determined, if possible, to ascertain the true state of their affairs.

She found too soon that Sir Vincent had contracted debts to a much greater amount than she was able to disemburse, and by the advice of her early friend Michael Wright, she resolved to immediately discharge her attendants, sell the household effects, and, after having settled so many of them as she was able, to proceed at once to the country. This resolve was quickly acted upon, but a few days having passed away ere Fanny, accompanied by Michael Wright and her darling boy, who was now in the seventh year of his age, were on the way to their place of her birth—the dear old farm house, as she (Fanny) so often called it. At length they neared their journey's end, the sun was fast sinking behind the western hills as they approached the village by way of a narrow lane, skirted thickly on either side with dwarf trees of various kinds. They now crossed a stile, which enabled them to obtain a distinct view of the farm house. A glowing fire kindled by some gipsies, and near which an old woman was seated, burnt brightly a short distance from them. This was, however, unnoticed by Fanny, who, gazing intently in the direction of her early home, falteringly exclaimed—

"Yes, there stands my birth-place, the dear old house I once called home ! What evil star prompted me to desert it ? Father, stern, unrelenting father, thy misguided, wretched child gazes on the abode that shelters thee, and trembles, for she dares not return to that once happy dwelling—she would die in its porch, and death would be bliss compared with thy stern look, and the sound of thy voice teeming with curses ! Oh! I have merited that curse, but I must not hear it from thy lips. No, no, heaven in its mercy will spare me that trial ! Fool! what do I—I here then ? Yes, yes, 'twas to gaze once more on this spot, and hear from some strange rustic. that—that all I love are well and happy."

At this moment Michael, who, being unwilling for a time to disturb Fanny, had wandered on a short distance with the boy, returned; and leading young Vincent to his mother said—

"There be thy mother, boy; go kiss her, and doant'ee sob no more."

"Dear—dear mamma !" faltered Vincent.

" My bright, my blooming boy !" cried Fanny, embracing him fondly, " why, there are tears in thy blue eyes: silly child, to weep—there, your mother will kiss the tear-drops dry. Yes, dear image of my—my only love, thou hast no birth-right but thy mother's heart—that will be ever thine while she tarries on the earth. Born to splendid competence, and stripped of it by thy prodigal parents !—tell me, when you with your play-mates seek the village church-yard to pluck the wild-flower or, gambol o'er the graves of those who sleep there, should you mark a rude mound, without a stone to tell the dead one's name, many a voice will tell you whose it is—they'll speak of your lowly state, your blighted fortune ! Oh, do not then, in the bitterness of yonr beggared hope, lift your young hands to curse her !"

" Whom, whom, dear mother ?"

" Your wretched, guilty mother."

" Never !—never !" cried Vincent, affectionately.

" My—my own, my dearest," sobbed Fanny, in a tone of the deepest pathos.

" I—I be shot if I can stand this," ejaculated the sympathizing Michael ; " if they go on at this rate, I—I shall blubber like a bull. Doant'ee, Miss —Madam, I mean—it's too cutting for human nature to stand up against! It's all very well for women and babbies, but—but its so unmannerly to catch a great hulk of a fellow like I, a—a snivelling !" and the honest fellow dashed away an unbidden tear.

" There—there," said Fanny, striving to appear calm—" to thy home, go, go—I—I will tarry yet a brief space that—that I may glut my vision by a longer gaze upon this—this much-loved scene—but—but I'll shed no tear—I'll breathe no sigh for that which is now hopeless. Go, go."

" Bless'ee—bless'ee," faltered Michael, " but doant'ee stay long, Miss —Madam, I mean—I—I shall be eat up wi' a million fears ! I ax pardon —but if thee knew how anxious—how very anxious will be my heart till we again meet—thee wouldn't stay a minute. Now brighten up and be brisk, thee need'st summat to strengthen thee, so I'll away home and pre-pare thee summat warm and comfortable, and, bless'ee, don't'ee let it get cold. Come along, young Squire !" So saying, Michael Wright took young Vincent by the hand, and proceeded slowly towards the cottage.

" Squire, indeed," ejaculated Fanny bitterly, as she watched their de-parture, " that title died with thy father. Poor beggared innocent ! But I—I must be brief, I will not vex that honest heart by unnecessary delay —a few moments to contemplate this scene ere I leave to see it perhaps no more. There is the old stile where we so oft have met. Fly these thoughts of the dead, let me dwell only on the living—I—I would give half my wretched life could I but see my sister here alone ; her—her beautiful eyes might flash with anger, but oh ! like the glorious sun-shine after a shower, how dear the ray that would follow it—the tone of her voice—the fond profession of her sweet love. Ah ! what form is that which breaks through the gloom ? Some one comes at last to tell of those whom my heart longs so much to hear."

A tall form was rapidly approaching by way of the narrow lane, and, whoever it might be, appeared to be merry, occasionally giving careless utterance to snatches of various songs, one of which was overheard by Fanny and ran thus :—

> "The bird has flown to its nest in the tree,
> So come pretty maiden and ramble with me,
> The sun it has sunk, and the stars beam bright,
> The time for love's song is the still hour of night!
>> Come, come, pretty maiden, come, come."

"I've heard that voice, that song before," ejaculated Fanny. "Ah, I remember now; 'tis 'Dark David,' as he is called, that wild and reckless man. He comes by the path to the village inn—I will not meet him," and she hid herself among the bushes, which she considered would prove a sufficient place of security till he had passed. Again she heard the voice "Come, come, pretty maiden with me!"

"It's a matter of astonishment to me," continued Dark Davy, "the sweet notes of my voice or my prepossessing appearance don't win any of the pretty faces in these parts! Ah, it's an abominable prejudice they've taken against me, and all for what, I should like to know? Because once on a time they took it in their wise heads to clap me in the county-jail, only for indulging in a little innocent pastime—snaring a few dozen hares, and popping at a partridge or so! It's what I call a burning shame."

He now placed his head between a gap in the bushes a few yards from where Fanny had taken refuge, and opposite the exact spot where the gipsies' fire before spoken of still burnt brightly. After a moment or two he shouted—

"Hallo, old Mother Devildum! are you asleep still? I can hear the old pot biling over.—Shake your feathers, you lazy old warmint, do!—I wants my supper."

"That is not all you want!" cried the old woman, rising from behind the fire—it's not the hour yet—our brothers are abroad. Vermin, did you say?—I could *hang* you, vermin as I am!"

"Hang! ho, ho, ho!" laughed Davy, in a hoarse voice.

"Aye, laugh on," cried the hag, "your note will change ere the next day dawns, when you will be shut from the light, and the limbs that are now free will then be fettered!"

"Why you old witch," roared Davy, "what shall I do to *arn* the darbies?"

"A deed—a dark deed," rejoined the woman mysteriously; "a—a deed that if fulfilled will place the hangman's noose around you! Wait but a moment, and I'll tell you what you would do; come nearer, and I'll breathe it in your ear."

David approached, and the sybil said—

"You would do a deed of darkness—a deed of robbery and—and MURDER!"

"Almighty powers! what am I doomed to hear?" whispered Fanny, who had been listening intently to the preceding dialogue between Dark Davy and the gypsey sybil.

"What's that?" cried Davy, starting.

"The echo of your trembling heart—the inward voice that none but the guilty ever hear!" said the gypsey. "Does the vermin speak true?" she continued.

"How, in the name of the devil, did the old hag learn my secret?" muttered Davy. "I must win her over to my plan. Hollo! Mabel, *my* sweetest, come nearer the bushes and I'll let you into the secret; I would

THE CONVENT OF ST. FREDRICA

# EMELINE;
OR,
## THE LOVE PLEDGE.

man gave utterance to a piercing cry and immediately fell dead at his feet.

"Damnation!" roared Uberto "are ten of ye insufficient where I alone could have gained a victory? off—off ye hinds, or I may also become your enemy!"

"I—I choke—tear him a—way—away," gasped the man Sir Gilbert had drawn down with him, "he—ee tears my—my—"

At this moment a bullet whizzed in among them—the aim had been taken with fatal accuracy, and Sir Gilbert writhed in mortal agony.

"I—I have him still," he gasped "still—still, e—ven in—in death—will I—torment him—I—I will never release my—my gripe—never—never!"

"Why don't you tear him from me?" again ejaculated the prostrate robber in a kind of hissing whisper—"my—my breath grows short—l—I———

"Is it an object of such little moment to see a comrade murdered?" shrieked Uberto foaming with rage, "pierce your enemy to the heart's core!"

Still the robbers stood irresolute; each superstitiously imagined their present enemies possessed superhuman power, and as such dreaded their task.

"The recreants dare not move—they know a greater power then we possess operates against them!" cried Sir Calthart; and again he rushed forward, reckless alike of death, or danger.

The savage nature of the robbers at length seemed to resume its wonted sway, and our hero would have fallen beneath their ire, had not Uberto interfered to save him.

"Leave this rash hind to linger in hopeless captivity," said he; "and since ye once more seem actuated by your former spirit, look to your fallen comrade."

All were now as eager to obey as they were before irresolute, and, approaching the inanimate form of Sir Gilbert, endeavored to place their comrade on his feet.

"But, H—ll," roared one, "the dead man still clutches firmly; see—see—I—I cannot make him let go his hold."

A low gurgling was heard in the robber's throat;

"You 'll be too late! sever the hand—quick," cried Uberto—"quick—quick."

One of them was about to do so, but immediately shrunk back aghast.

"Oh God!" he cried, "I—I cannot—the corpse seems starting to life!"

"Fool!" vociferated the chieftain.

"I—I may be," returned the man, "but mark me—I wouldn't touch that hand for all the wealth of Peru."

"Nor I," said another, "'twould haunt me for ever! sleeping or waking I should still feel its cold, clammy touch."

"Then I shouldn't! so stand back, ye superstitious hounds!" roared Caspero, roughly approaching, and the next moment the hand of Sir Gilbert, being severed from the wrist, fell with a dull sound to the floor."

"You have not sufficient courage to cast the hand forth," cried one of the fellows who had been taunted with the appellative of a "superstitious hound."

"*Indeed!*" sneered the man thus challenged to the performance of an act, at which he felt not the slightest repugnance, and picking up the severed hand, upon one of the fingers of which was a diamond ring of great beauty, he cried—

"Here is a matchless gem. Mark ye! I claim it as a trophy of having perfomed an act at which my *brave comrades* shuddered!" So saying the remorseless man of blood tore off the ring, and, approaching the window, threw up the casement. "Hence!" he cried, as, with a jerk, he endeavored to cast the hand forth; but to his horror it clove to him as firmly as though it were fastened by a cord.

"This act of sacrilege will bring thee to the tomb," cried one, who, terrified at the strangeness of the event, sped from the room.

Uberto, desirous of seeing his remaining captive well secured, had already taken his departure, and there being now no restraint on the acts of his ruthlessm yrmidons, the remainder of them quitted the apartment, leaving the ruffian to the torture of the dead hand, of which he had no power to dispossess himself. Left to himself, Caspero gazed wildly around him; the arm of the murdered Sir Gilbert still lay across the throat of him who had become the victim of his deadly gripe, and a short distance farther on was the lifeless forms of the two men slain by Sir Calthart Burgoyne.

"Oh, God!" cried the unwilling tenant of this horrid chamber of death, who was afraid to turn his eyes from St. Clair, "oh, God! he—he would strangle *me*—but—but he is dead—ha! ha! dead—dead!" Again he tried to shake off the hand, his eyes protruded, and his lips were colorless. "I—I shall conquer ye—yet!" he groaned.

In his endeavors to accomplish his desire he had again reached the open casement but turning suddenly round, the glazed eyes of Sir Gilbert—which were wide open—met his terrified glare. Now his agitated mind was tortured by a recollection of the warning he had received when returning from the vaults beneath the castle—" As I am, ere the setting of another sun—so wilt thou be." This greatly increased his fright, and in all the agonies of hopeless despair he cried—

"Off—off; I—I will crush thee!" and he unconsciously advanced, but again started back with horror. "He—he comes—he comes!" he ejaculated, literally foaming with madness. "Away—away! I—I—no matter—victory! victory!" and for the last time approaching the inanimate object of his fears he fell lifeless beside it.

---

## CHAP. IX.

### TRIUMPH OF VILLANY—THE BURNING CASTLE—PERILOUS DESCENT.

Having well secured his prisoner, and maddened with rage at the loss his band had sustained, Uberto sought Freeman, to whom he related what had been overheard by Caspero in the forest.

"The number of our enemies are great," said he.

"No matter" returned Freeman; "we have already overthrown their two general's which renders their complete destruction easy, comparative with what it might otherwise have been."

"How then wouldst thou advise me to act?" asked Uberto.

"How?" echoed Freeman. Array one of the band in a garb resembling that worn by our prisoner, and, when night approaches let him hie to the battlements. In the interim our cannon must be stationed so as to face the drawbridge."

"What then?"

"Let each man be ready with his match, and, as our foes advance, the pretended minstrel must give the signal they will be so anxious to hear. Being thus deceived they will approach without caution;—fire into the midst of them—the result is obvious;"

"It is!" cried Uberto; "they'll soon sleep in death! ha—ha! to the ramparts, on—on!"

\* \* \* \* \* \* \* \* \*

As the deep-toned bell of the convent boomed forth the hour of nine, the gallant followers of Sir Calthart—preceded by the abbot Francesco, issued forth, and halted on the glade before it.

"My heart is oppressed by strange forebodings," ejaculated Francesco; "but should harm befall any of you—which Holy Mary forbid—that your souls may rest in peace is my most earnest prayer." Pausing to dash away an unbidden tear, he in a loud, but solemn cadence, pronounced the usual Catholic benedicite, and the knights departed. Proceeding to the tower, the holy father watched their movements by the faint light of the moon. At length the umbrageous foliage of the forest trees screened them from his gaze, and he hastened to join the brotherhood at their nightly devotions. The Almanza ruins were at length gained, and although the moon, which had hitherto enrobed their path in a girdle of silver now became screened by a dark cloud passing over it they could plainly discern the glimmering of a torch on the ramparts. This all surmised was borne by Sir Calthart Burgoyne, and breathlessly awaited his signal. It was heard, and an immediate rush made across the drawbridge, when their astonished ears were assailed by the thundering echoes of Uberto's cannon, which felled many to the earth.

"Treachery! treachery!" shouted one who had escaped the fatal bullets; "away with ye!—to the wood—the wood!"

But few, however, had sufficient time to retreat; Uberto's well-tutored myrmidons had dexterously contrived to re-load, and a second volley from their destructive instruments of death, swept many more of them away. The few who still remained unscathed leapt upon their steeds, and urging them to their utmost speed, dashed into the wood.

The Robbers were now about to quit the castle. To their surprise, however, the whole building was enveloped in a dense volume of black smoke, the cause of which soon became apparent; it was on fire, and vast sheets of lurid flame burst forth from every door and window around. What was to be done? Escape by the proper outlets was impossible, and the hissing flames threatened speedy death. Uberto's guilty mind was pierced by a maddening recollection of the singular import of the mystic warning, which he feared was about to be most horribly ratified. At this juncture, one of the ruffians discovering a long coil of rope on the ramparts, cried—

"Saved, saved! fasten this to one of the cannons and let us descend—quick!—quick, I say, or, by h—ll, we shall all be roasted alive!"

The rope was soon firmly secured to one of the guns, still hot from recent use, and Uberto was about to descend into what now formed but a swampy marsh, but had formerly been the bed of the moat. A piercing cry of anguish, however, uttered by some one near him, caused him for a moment to defer his intention, and he shuddered as, on turning round, he discovered one of his myrmidons writhing in agony. A quantity of lead upon the battlement above (some of which had fallen upon him) was rapidly melting, and poured down in various places like a bright flood of liquid silver.

"Indecision is death!" vociferated the chieftain; follow me quick!" and the next moment he was suspended between heaven and earth, by the rope. At length all alighted without further accident, and, creeping from the ditch, sought their steeds, and dashed into the forest. They soon lost sight of the castle, though for miles they could distinguish a ray of crimson, that plainly revealed where stood the scene of their late carnage!

---

## CHAP. X.

THE SECRET DOOR—MIRACULOUS ESCAPE OF EMELINE AND HER LOVER.

Upon reaching the castle, Emeline was conducted to the subterraneous passages which led from thence to the forest. These contained a number of vaults built of solid masonry, some of which (when occasion required) were used by the band as a place of rendezvous or concealment. The dreariness of this singular abode tended considerably towards increasing her wretchedness. Luckily, however, she was placed under the fostering care of the wife of one of the robbers named Maude, in whom we have to recognise an exception to the ancient adage that 'evil communications corrupt good morals' for although the wife of an outlaw, the kind, gentle

# GARDEN OF ROMANCE.

—

## FANNY GREENWELL;

OR,

### THE OLD FARM HOUSE.

be gallant enough to come over to you, only I'm waiting for one that musn't be missed !"

"What horrid secret am I about to hear?" again ejaculated Fanny, peering cautiously from her place of concealment; perhaps heaven ordains me to be the instrument to save the doomed being, whose death is planning in yon villain's thought—I will listen but—but not stir—not even breathe."

"Dos't watch thy fellow's coming?" asked Mabel, observing that Davy was gazing somewhat anxiously down the lane.

"Aye, Mabel," said Davy; "a plague on the snail, where tarries he?"

"Despair not," rejoined the sybil, "he will be here full soon to aid thee in thy hellish work !"

"Why Mabel, how uncommon unfeminine you are getting," laughed Davy; "what an expression from one of the *fair* sex."

"Fair !" echoed Mabel, "do not gibe one; I court not flattery, I love best the truth.   My skin is dyed by the hot sun and curling smoke of the wood-fire," continued she, laying her hand on her heart; "but I thank the Great Master, all is fair and pure here!   Would I could say as much of those with whom destiny forces me to mingle."

"Come, no preaching," growled Davy; you know my purpose you say?"

"Know it! aye, as well as if 'twere breathed from your own lips—I'll tell it, and you shall own I speak the truth :—A good and just man did you (as you deemed) an injury—"

"True !" interrupted Davy, "an injury from which I never freed myself; he blackened my name, all who were honest shunned me; he made me what I am – a wandering vagabond; but we shall be even soon—very soon!"

"Thou wouldst take his life?" cried Mabel.

"No, I seek not that," said Davy, "I only covet the means that sweetens it—his—his gold!"

"Do not deny it," said Mabel, "there is *One* that hears you, who reads your inmost heart and knows the truth! Oh, banish that black thought, let not the curse of the orphan and the needy follow you. Oh, spare the life that exists alone for acts of love and charity; let him pass freely with his gold—he treasures it to make his children happy, to help the aged and the needy, who cannot help themselves!"

"I tell you again I seek not his life," said Davy; "be silent, and hear me; I'll not deceive thee, Mabel; hang it, don't look so doubtingly—tonight he meets, at the 'King's Head,' a young farmer, who wishes to buy the lease of his farm. He has thriven in the world, and would buy a better to bestow on the husband of his daughter and their children—"

"Whom you would make homeless," interposed Mabel. Must your hate fall on the innocents who never harmed you? Shame on thee, if thou art man! David, this deed must not, *shall* not be done!"

"Peace, woman," cried David hoarsely; "I—I have sworn it!—deeply sworn it by the ashes of my mother, whose heart was broken by the miseries *he* heaped upon her son!—Yes, mother," he continued, "the—the outcast owes your memory a love that the whole world can never destroy!—Mabel, you bring to my sight her wan face, the sunken eyes I saw floating in tears, the cold clammy touch of death as her wasted hand pressed that of her truant son. I—I have never shed a single tear since I stood beside her pauper-grave! Hear me and be dumb—by the soul of the mother who loved me, the—the gold of Greenwell shall be mine, aye, and if fate so wills it—his—his blood—his blood!"

Fanny, who was horror-struck at what she just heard, gave utterance to a piercing shriek.

"Whence that sound?" cried Davy, who was about to examine the bushes, but was prevented by the sound of voices which proceeded from some peasants who were rapidly approaching.

"Ah! there are men approaching," said he, in a tone of alarm. Plunge through the thicket, Mabel; down—down into the dell and hide till they have passed us!"

So saying, Dark Davy leapt across the embankment, and seizing the aged prophetess round the waist, dashed into an adjoining thicket with as much ease as though his burthen were less than the weight of a child.

Feeling assured they were now far away, and that she was perfectly safe, Fanny came from her hiding place, and, falling on her knees on the green sward, cried—

"Blessed be the hour I returned to the home of my father; heaven hath sent me back to save him. Joy!—joy! joy—Ha, ha, ha!—It—it will gain me his love, and a treasure dearer far, his—his pardon—his pardon! Ha, ha, ha!"

As the sounds of that hysterical laugh died away on the air, the peasants, whose voices had alarmed Davy, crossed the stile.

"If ye are men—if ye are fathers—husbands," cried Fanny, "if ye own parents that are dear to you, do—do not stay to question me, but guide my footsteps to an inn called the ' King's Head,' there's a life depending on your speed ! on—on !''

The peasants were amazed at the wild appearance of Fanny, but made no comments.

" This way," cried one, " follow !"

" God bless you," retorted Fanny. " Father, dear father, you will be saved—saved ! Your child returns to warn you ! Come, come," and she rushed hastily onward towards the village.

## CHAP. IX.

### THE KING'S HEAD.—FATHER AND DAUGHTER.—DEPARTURE OF GREENWELL.

Farmer Greenwell, accompanied by George Rutly, had already reached the ' King's Head,' at which place they were soon joined by the young farmer mentioned by Dark Davy as the expected purchaser of the Briar's Farm. This transaction being disposed of satisfactorily to all parties, the purchaser quitted the hostel. As he departed, George Rutly, gazing on the old man with looks of gratitude, said—

" This last act of kindness almost robs me of the power to acknowledge it—words are too weak ; my wife shall thank you with tears of joy."

" No, we'll have no tears," said Greenwell, " her eye shall beam with happiness ; if I see that, I am well repaid—and after all, for what ? An act of duty—a duty, dear to a fond father's heart. Your prosperity, and that of your children, is the only wish left the desolate and deserted old man now."

" Deserted, sir !" echoed George, but immediately calling to mind the flight of Fanny, he continued—" Pardon me, I had forgot !"

" But I *never* can," cried Greenwell; " till I cease to exist, remembrance can only die with me."

" Talk not of dying, sir ;" said George, " you will live long to bless us."

" That blessings may shower on you, I pray Heaven," rejoined Greenwell. " But the night has set ; away with you to the steward at the Hall, say (if the good old Squire's health permit) in the morning we'll wait on him to tender the purchase money and receive the lease."

" Shall not I be your companion home, sir ?" asked George.

" No," returned Greenwell, " I should but impede your speed—cross the five-acre field and the little bridge by the mill-dam, it will save you at least half your distance. Be speedy, as I shall be home long before you."

" I will, I will," said George, as, with a light heart, he bounded out of the apartment. The farmer being now alone gazed through the half-opened casement—all was calm and beautiful without, " and the world wore the starry darkness round her, like a girdle spangled with gems."

" Yes, Sophy," he said, soliloquising ; " my best and dearest, you will guide your innocent children in the right path, and when you come to join your old father in the grave, you will descend there calm and content, knowing you have left behind a competence for them to buffet with the frowns of a harsh world. But oh, should there be a rebel in your little flock, heaven snatch it from you in its childhood; better to mourn it dead, than dishonored like mine, the heartlesss one!"

At this moment the voice of Fanny was heard without.

"Here, here, say you?" she cried, addressing those who had guided her thither.

Greenwell started. "Ah! that voice! hushed be its tone; to me it is hateful. Let me begone!" he vociferated, and he was about to quit the house, but his passage was stopped by Fanny who threw herself at his feet.

"Parricide! let me pass; I will not know thee—let me pass!" he shouted.

"'Twill be to die—to fall by the murderer's hand; the crafty plotter waits to take thy life! Oh, father—wronged father! your penitent, heart-broken, disobedient child hath been sent by heaven to save thee!"

"What mockery is this?"—Do not hope to forge a tale to impress on a heart of flint—let me pass!"

"To thy grave," groaned Fanny; "Oh, spurn—even curse me, but, for the love of life, I entreat thee to hear me!"

"I own no love of life, for you, viper, poisoned its joy! What is life to me, when I must feel its inheritance is shame! Look at me if you can —a brief seven years have passed since you left me a hale and hearty man —the snows of premature old age were not then upon my head, nor was the cheek hollowed, or the heart sad. No, it was light and buoyant. Here is your work; look up and shudder at the wreck—the ruin you have made!"

"I cannot meet your look of anger, for my eyes are sightless with their tears. I deceived, disobeyed you; I forfeited all—a father's and a sister's love—I, imprudent and misguided as I was, gave all to one, who is now no more!"

"Dead?" said Greenwell, with a shudder.

"Yes, he is in the grave, and the widowed heart returns to those who propped it in its helplessness. For heaven's love spurn not the lonely and the dying, for *I* am dying, father; I shall not trouble you long—the earth will soon hide her, who is so much hated!" Greenwell covered his eyes with his hands. "A tear?" sobbed Fanny. "Blessed, blessed drop—it hath fallen on my burning heart like the dew of heaven on the sun-burnt flower. Oh, do not look so stern; let the outpourings of your heart be shed on the head of your penitent child—I never saw you weep before!"

"Tears have fallen, though you saw them not," said Greenwell. "What were your father's tears to you? You were smiling in the halls of pampered pride, gay, happy, nor even gave a thought to those you had deserted!"

"Oh, do not think me quite so heartless. In the solitude of night, the sleepless truant thought of her home and of those she left behind her; and when sleep blessed her, she dreamt that they were happy. I saw you plainly in my vision, but your dark hair had not turned so silvery white, the brightness of your eye had not faded. Oh, let it speak to your heart, father, as it does to mine—'twas she, Fanny, caused all this, and ask again if Fanny does not *feel* it?"

"The unthinking mariner, who steers the rich bark upon the rock, may sorrow for the wreck his rashness might have spared," said Greenwell;

# EMELINE;
OR,
## THE LOVE PLEDGE.

spirit she ever possessed previous to her connection with them, was still her chief characteristic. A ray of pleasure ever illumined her beautiful countenance, and the bewitching smile that played o'er her glowing cheeks, plainly revealed the soul that reigned within. It was near midnight, and Emeline who had been offering up her usual nightly devotions to the Great Giver of life, previous to seeking her second night's repose at this her miserable prison-house, was greatly surprised at beholding her kind companion gazing towards her with a fixed look of undefinable intensity, and who at length exclaimed—

"Thy unrighteous captivity troubles me, lady, sorely troubles me : but say, could I manage to convey thee from hence, wouldst thou ever betray me ?"

"*Betray* thee ? never, as I hereafter hope for mercy !—never—never!"

Placing her hand upon an iron bar, that was hidden by a cotton hanging, Maude partially contrived to remove it from its fastening ; suddenly, however, it slipped from her grasp, producing a crash that echoed throughout the whole building.

"Confusion!" muttered Maude; "my clumsiness will ruin all—hark !" Some one was rapidly approaching,

"Be seated!" whispered Maude, "quick! stir not, nor appear discomposed, or we are lost—aye, lost beyond all hope, all—all."

"Whence came that sound ?" cried a rough voice ; the next moment the door was thrown back, and in stalked one of the robbers.

"How dare ye thus break our privacy?" demanded Maude.

"Whence that sound, I say?" retorted the fellow evasively; "did ye not hear it?"

"Aye, truly did we!" rejoined Maude, "still that argueth not that we can define its source, but mark! thou hadst better retire, or thou'lt have cause to repent thee of thy rashness."

"Indeed!" growled the fellow, looking suspiciously around the apartment. Nothing wrong, however, met his gaze, and bidding them a rough 'good-night' he again stalked away.

Maude, who appeared to breathe more freely, again applied herself energetically to her task. The bar was at length removed, when, throwing back a small door, she desired Emeline to take the lamp and follow her. After threading their way through a number of dismal passages, they turned an angle of the wall, and struck into a large vaulted cavern.

"Somewhere about the northern side of this cave," said Maude, "is an iron plate, which we must discover ere we can obtain egress. Hold forth the light."

Emeline obeyed; but the flickering flame of the lamp seemed but to add an additional gloom, and they were reduced to the alternative of groping their way along by the damp walls. Having found the plate, they pressed a kind of button which was attached to its centre, and it immediately revolved on its axis, disclosing a gap sufficiently large to admit of their passing through. Having so done, Emeline found they had entered the dungeon into which Uberto had cast Sir Calthart, who was now reposeing on a straw pallet in one corner thereof. His whole frame seemed convulsed. With an affectionate look of pity, our heroine raised his head, and whispered in his ear:—

"Calthart! dear Calthart—thy Emeline bids the rise—awake!"

The effect was magical; he opened his fine sparkling orbs, and started to his feet, but he was again drawn suddenly back with a violent jerk.

"Oh God!—I—I forget my chains," he faltered. "They do well to secure me thus! Having tested the power of my just resentment, they dread its force!"

"Of a verity, do they," said Maude, who having disappeared for the last few moments, now re-entered the dungeon, disguised in the habit of a page. Taking a key from her vest, she freed the young knight from his manacles, and the lovers rushed into each others embrace. Maude looked on with pleasure, but, knowing that 'delays are dangerous,' she hinted the propriety of a speedy departure.

"The ordeal is not yet passed," said she, "as we cannot depart from hence without passing through the cave occupied by the robbers!"

"Then are we indeed lost," sighed Emeline.

"Nay, exercise due caution and fear not," said Maude. "The outlaws, who have been drinking deeply, are enlocked in sleep—see!" So saying, she threw open a small door which led into a kind of circular vault or cave, which they entered.

"You see theirs is not always a bed of roses," whispered Maude; "but they sleep soundly, nevertheless." And stepping upon a ladder that reached an aperture in the roof, she beckoned to them to follow, and immediately disappeared.

Observing a sword lying near one side of the cave, Calthart seized it, and joyously hurried forth with his companion. At length they reached the forest. The azure firmament was studded with glittering gems; and a gentle zephyr that played o'er the heated brow of Calthart partly soothed the bitter anguish arising from his late captivity.

"A mile or two hence stands a small cottage belonging to a forrester named Edric," said Maude, addressing her companions; "Having oft befriended him, he will doubtless give us a shelter till the morrow; we can then venture forth with less fear of meeting any of the band. Shall we proceed thither?"

"We place ourselves entirely at thy disposal," said Calthart; "lead on."

The command was promptly obeyed, and in less than an hour they reached the cottage, where they obtained some refreshment, consisting of hot milk, which was served to them by the dame, whilst Edric was enjoying the fumes of his tobacco-pipe in the chimney corner. At day-break they again journeyed onwards. Reaching the convent of St. Fredrica, Sir Calthart applied his hand to the bell. At this moment he heard his name shouted by some one from behind, and on turning round he discovered Uberto and his lieutenant Freeman rapidly approaching. All gave themselves up for lost, but the priory-gate rolled back on its hinges, and they were scarcely within the portal, ere it was firmly secured.

"Fools!" shouted Uberto, as he reached the spot, "ye have given me a kindly notice of your hiding place, from whence I can now drag ye at my pleasure.—Ha—ha—ha!"

Followed by Freeman, he made all possible speed to obtain the assistance of the residue of his band. Nor were the inmates of the priory more tardy in adopting measures to defeat the attack they well knew would soon be made upon them. A violent ring was at length heard.

"They come—they come!" vociferated Calthart, addressing the few brave fellows who had escaped the fatal bullets on the night of their dreadful defeat at Almanza Castle. "Now my friends, remember, that 'unity is strength,' and meet them as they deserve. You will then avenge the cause of your murdered comrades, and deck your brows with laurels that never fade!"

Again the bell gave evidence of the impatience of their visitors.

"How, now?" cried the Abbot, proceeding to the gate; what means this disturbance?"

"You have strangers here," answered Uberto.

"I have—What then?" rejoined Francesco.

"I *demand* them of thee!" said the outlaw, in a tone of sarcasm.

"Fool!" cried the Abbot, who, giving utterance to a taunting laugh, left Uberto to brood upon the insult.

"To action—to action!" he cried, foaming with rage:—"Tear down the gate!—quick my men! quick, quick!"

Giving a yell of triumph, the Outlaws obeyed the mandate. The rusty hinges offered but slight opposition, and, with a tremendous crash down—down it went.

"Onward!" shouted Uberto, "and, mark me—shew no mercy, or I henceforth become your most deadly enemy! On I say!"

Their ears were again assailed by the taunting laugh of Francesco. This was immediately followed by a loud volley of musketry, which, like a mighty pestilence that bears down all before it, launched most of them into eternity.   But two only were they, who still retained the frail thread of existence! one of these was Uberto, who had received several severe wounds, and as he now lay, writhing in agony, both mental and bodily, he again distinctly heard the following words—

> " Thy name—thy hands are stain'd with blood,
> Thy deeds are stamp'd with the curse of God ;
> This night—but I must say no more,
> Uberto, Uberto ! thy reign's nigh o'er !"

He now beheld the fair form of a female standing before him, upon whom he gazed with astonishment.   A slight convulsion seemed to possess him, as with an eagle-like glance he scanned her every feature, which appeared familiar to him, though he at length exclaimed—

" Who art thou, that giveth utterance to words of such fearful import ?"

" One whom thou long since imagined in the grave !"

" The grave !—who talks of graves ?" said Uberto, whose senses now wandered, " Let weddings be the theme, I'll have a bridal—aye, a bridal !"

" Thou'rt already wedded to the grave !" said the lady ; " thy sun of life is fast·setting, and darkness—the sable mantle of death, hovers o'er thee."

" Darkness—death !   All is light—light as the mid-day sun, when its golden disk is unobscured by a single cloud—light as the sparkling snow-flake that enrobes the tree-bough in winter ! but I'd have wine !—bring me a goblet of rich rosy wine—ha—ha ! wine—wine ! it cheers the soul.'

Francesco—who, accompanied by the knights and several of the monks, had been listening with eager amaze to this extraordinary dialogue, invited the lady to enter the priory.   Uberto was carried to a chamber, whither she followed him, and seated herself by his bed-side.

" I would be alone till this unfortunate man is blest with returning consciousness, if Heaven wills it he ever should be," said she.

Her wish was complied with, and the chieftain fell into a deep slumber, from which he awoke considerably refreshed.   Again he beheld the mysterious prophetess, as he supposed her, and again enquiring who she was, received the same rejoinder as heretofore.

" One whom thou long since imagined in the grave !"

" Tell me, I conjure thee, mysterious being who and what thou art ?" gasped Uberto.

" Has time then so altered the countenance of one whom, with the breath of a parasite, thou hast often sworn to love, above all created beings, Lord Alfred of Almanza ?   Know then that she whom thou once called thy Eleanor—thy—thy wife ! stands before thee !"

" My—my Eleanor—my wife !   God of Heaven, 'tis impossible !"

" Nay, thou shalt have proof—I will bring before thee scenes of by-gone days, in which thou acted !—Scenes of m—murder—and of blood !"

Ringing a bell that stood upon a table, Sir Calthart Burgoyne and Francesco entered the room.   She desired them to be seated and attend to certain disclosures she was about to make concerning Uberto, and which were of the utmost importance.   Her desire being promptly complied with, she immediately commenced the following

### NARRATIVE.

" The real name of the outlaw, who now suffers from the hand of retributive justice, and who I fervently pray will at length repent him of his iniquity, is Lord Alfred of Almanza."   Her auditors started.   " 'Twas

# GARDEN OF ROMANCE.

—

## FANNY GREENWELL;

### OR,

### THE OLD FARM HOUSE.

" so it is with thee.   Do not cling around me—to win my pardon now, is hopeless.   I will commune with myself, and if my heart can grant it, in time it shall be thine."   So saying he left the house.

" Ha, ha!   Joy—joy!" sobbed Fanny, who, having buried her face in her hands, had not noticed her father's departure.   " My heart is lightened of its load, for hope is dawning o'er it—Father!"   She now missed him.   " Ah, he has gone to die!" she shrieked, " to—to fall by the murderer's hand ere human power can save him!   Oh, God!—with what speed he wends his way—I must lose not a moment, or he is lost for ever!" and she rushed in pursuit of him with the speed of an antelope.

---

## CHAP. X.

### THE CONCLUSION.

Having nearly overtaken him, she saw Dark Davy spring from a thicket and present a loaded pistol at his head.

" Father, dear father," she cried, " beware of thy enemy!—He comes —he comes!"

" Gold—gold," muttered Dark Davy who was about to fire; but at this critical moment Michael Wright, who, alarmed at the long absence of Fanny, was now seeking her, leapt across the stile and, seizing him by the throat, brought him to the earth.

No. 9.

" Dang thee down for a wicked toad as thou art," he cried.   " Ah, thee may struggle, but thee mun be plaguy strong if thee slips the grip o' Michael Wright !"

" Michael Wright !" echoed Davy ;  " what, foiled again by *thee ?*"

" Ah, thee knows me, dost thee ?" said Michael ; " hold up thee ugly black muzzle, and lets ha' a peep at thee.   Why, I be shot if it aint the poaching chap I ha' a tussel wi' when I wur gamekeeper at the Hall.— Oh, thee hast a hankering for thy old quarters, hast thee ?   Away wi' him, lads, to jail."

This last sentence was addressed to some peasants whom the noise had attracted to the spot, and who eagerly did as they were desired.   Fanny now approached her father.

" By the memory of my mother—by the remembrance of those days when you watched your children's helplessness," said she, " I pray thee have pity.   I grovel in the dust before you ; trample on me—spurn me— I'll bear it all without a murmur, let me but hear the blessed sound of pardon !"

" Pardon !—do not hope to win it," said Greenwell ; " my heart to all mankind is still the same—to thee it is impenetrable.   Begone, thou hast planted furrows on my cheek—cast shame on my white hairs—almost broken the heart that would have bled to foster thee.   Woman, begone ; I know thee not.   Seek ye to mingle among the children of chastity—to poison the innocent mind—to sow the rancorous seed, the fruit of which must render fathers, mothers, kindred wretched !   Seek your home in the gay world—Greenwell of the Briars Farm, knows not the paramour of Vincent Melville !"

" Vincent Melville !" echoed a voice.   The next moment the gypsey sybil approached.   " Vincent Melville !   Oh, speak that name again !" che cried ; " it is the herald-note that speaks of joy and bliss to come !"

" Alas ! 'twas Vincent Melville, who lured me from my home, who snatched me from my father's love by means of a secret marriage !" sighed fanny.   " 'Twas Vincent Melville who deceived, destroyed me !"

" No, he did *not* deceive you," said Mabel.

" How, what meanest thou ?" retorted Greenwell.

" *Behold !*" cried Mabel, holding forth a scrap of paper ; " here, here is the proof ; the hand that gave it is mouldered now."

" From whom did you receive it ?" enquired Fanny.

" Mortimer !"

" Him ! the mock priest who joined us ?"

" Nay, wrong not his memory—he wore the holy robe and never lost it— that was his dying confession ; and men, with the last words lingering on their lips, love not untruths !"

" How came you possessed of this ?" asked Greenwell.

" He gave it to my care in a distant land on his death bed, " answered Mabel, " and I have never heard the name of Melville till now, though I have prayed to hear it night and day !"

" The hand of heaven is in this !" sobbed Fanny, throwing herself at her father's feet.

" No, not at my feet ! here, to the heart's core, " cried Greenwell ! " that desolate heart, that has not known a gleam of joy for many a day !" and folding her in his arms, he burst into a passion of tears.

" Ha, ha, huzza ! huzza !" shouted Michael, capering about like one beside himself, " I knew we should all be happy once again—huzza—huzza !"

" Huzza !—huzza !" echoed Mat Maythorn, who, approaching, said—" Allow me to introduce in the person o' the late Becky Wibbles, the present Mrs. Matty Maythorn."

" While I take a buss o' thy bride, run back to my cottage and fetch the young Squire," said Michael.

" Bless'ee, we've brought him with us," returned Mat ; " see !"

Crossing the hedge, he quickly returned, leading young Vincent, who, running to his mother, was by her placed in the arms of his grandfather.

" Heyday, the whole village have heard the news !" vociferated Michael ; " Who comes over the stile ?"

'Twas George Rutly and his wife, who, bathed in tears, threw herself upon her sister's neck.

" If tears must be shed," said George, " let them spring from joy's fountain ! Here is the will of the old Squire of Melville, bequeathing to the male heirs of his son, the old Hall and all its vast possessions !"

" Dear Fanny, your sufferings are ended, and peace and riches await you !" said Sophy, affectionately.

" I heed them not," returned Fanny, " for the last few moments have brought me the richest gift the world could grant. It's not the costly hall of Melville—it's a treasure dearer far—a father's pardon !" Crossing to Michael Wright, she resumed—" Michael, I have proved thy honest heart, believe thy love—it shall not go unrewarded—not a word—there is a respect due to the memory of the dead ! Father, sister, brother (blessed titles), I'll seek no more the splendid hall—the gaudy gear—the din of flatterers—the blessing, dearest to my soul, will ever be the smiles that . cheer the happy hearth of

THE OLD FARM HOUSE.

J. HEATHER.

---

# THE RIVAL KINGS,

## OR

## THE MAGIC FISH.

The great public square of the kingdom of Chess was the scene of warfare between the rival kings, Ebony and Ivory—the subject of dispute being a magic fish, to which each professed an equal right. They at length agreed to decide to whom it should revert, by engaging in mortal combat, when their royal consorts threw themselves suddenly between them.

" Stop, sires, and deign to hear us," cried the Queen of Ivory. " We pray ye terminate these cruel wars ; let no more blood be shed for the possession of a simple fish !"

" The magic powers of this enchanted fish may not be underrated," said the King of Ivory.

" No," rejoined the other, " for to me, as a matter of right it belongeth.

" Liar ! 'tis false !"

" Insolent !   Did I ever in the field turn pale as thou ?   I *blacken* with disgust to see thee, now, *white* as thine own cowardice."

" My soul shall endure no more !   Soldiers, to arms !'

" Aye, to arms !"

" Stay one moment, sires," cried one of the Queens ; " my sister and myself alike enjoin ye.   Let the first stranger who shall seek our kingdom, impartial and unbiassed, end the question—whose yon fish shall be—whose it shall not."

" Agreed !" cried both, and the King of Ebony rejoined :—

" My trusty knight—with what good speed ye may, quick to our outer walls, begone ! and whatsoever traveller ye see, bring him straight before us !"

The knight soon returned, bringing with him a young man, whose hands were bound with black and white cords.

" Why am I offered this indignity ?" he cried.

" Ha ! who have we here ?" whispered the Queen of Ivory.

" How handsome," rejoined the other.   " Unbind the youth !"

" Illustrious ladies, deign to inform me to what good fortune I owe the supreme happiness of being dragged, like a criminal, to your gracious feet ?"

" Your presence here was necessary, to restore peace between two brothers— you are destined to be a sovereign judge."

" Between you ladies?   How they squeeze my hand !" muttered the youth aside.   The Queen of Ivory replied—

" You will have to adjudge—"

" The apple to the fairest ?" suggested he.

" No, sir ;" said the Queen of Ebony, gloomily.   " A fish to the most deserving."

" A Fish ! ha, ha ! what an idea !"

" Yes, remember the judgment must be perfectly impartial—no bribery !" said the fair Queen.   " Are these diamonds to your taste?" she added, taking a bracelet from her arm, and sliding it into his hand.

" What liberality !   I pronounce—"

" Stay ! remember justice !" said the other; " don't be too hasty in your verdict : not that I wish to influence you against your conscience; but this ring becomes you mightily," and she placed the gem on his finger.

" Than this, much more acceptable would be one little kiss."

" My wish is, certainly, to refuse; but for her husband's sake, an anxious woman is compelled to submit."

" That's very true," rejoined the other, also placing her cheek to receive one.

" This stranger—which is he ?" cried the King of Ivory, who had been engaged with his soldiers for the last few moments.   " Does he know the nature of the case ?"

" Perfectly !" said the youth.   " A fish is the object of dispute beween your majesties.   Suppose you were to divide it into two parts, and each monarch take an equal share."

" To divide the fish would be to deprive it of its magic power !"

" Oh ! then it's a magic fish of which you have been speaking ? the object of litigation should always be placed before the eyes of the judge."

" Certainly, bring hither the fish !"

" By way of evidence—what is the superhuman faculty of the creature ?"

" That of transporting, in an instant, any person placed upon his back, to the remotest distance desired by them."

" An idea strikes me !" muttered the youth aside.   " Attend sires !" he said.

" I am convinced that your majesties have an equal right to this precious talisman : before pronouncing the verdict, however, allow me to repeat a moral fable :—

" Where yonder waves are rolling, two friends an oyster chanced to find. Each strove to retain possession of the prize, but while the strife was raging some one approached, to whom they appealed for judgment.   He wisely awarded to each a shell, and himself consumed the oyster."   Thus I for ever end this unholy strife.'   So saying—he placed himself across the back of the magic fish, which instantly conveyed him to his home.

# EMELINE;
## OR,
## THE LOVE PLEDGE.

from his forefathers the ruined castle a few miles hence, and known as the 'Owlets haunt,' derived its title. He, also, was once its happy possessor; but becoming dissolute, crime and reckless extravagance consumed his patrimony, when he became the chief of that daring band which has rendered desolate so many hearts, and whose career of infamy and bloodshed is just closed. A year or two previous to this, though already united to her who now unburthens her heart by this dread recital, he became smitten with a beautiful, but wild young female, whose name was Ellen Dugarde. All my efforts to regain his love were unavailing, and I would oft retire to my chamber to mourn in solitude. Upon one of these occasions Lord Alfred entered an apartment adjoining mine—a light footstep followed his; the door was closed; and I distincly heard him exclaim—

I tell thee Ellen, I cannot now decide, but I will meet thee at the 'Hermit's-cave' to-morrow at noon, when thou shalt hear my decision!"

I had heard enough; throwing myself on a couch I fell into a broken and unrefreshing slumber. &ast; &ast; &ast; &ast; &ast;

The time having arrived for their projected meeting, I determined to watch them. With a heavy heart did I pursue my way towards the appointed spot; doubts and fears gained alternate dominion over my soul; and the idea that deceit—oh, horrible thought!—possessed the bosom of one, whose truth—whose constancy I valued above all else on earth, pierced me to the heart's core. When those we love are false—if, indeed, we truly love them—the result is bitter heart-rending sorrow—sorrow from which we often rashly seek refuge by becoming self-destroyers, staining the earth with blood which ought never to have been spilt. All things else may go wrong—the world may frown, and we heed it not—relations may deny and disown us, and we regard it not—the friend of our bosom may play us false, and we forget it—all, all may bestow upon us their ill-will—they may vilify—they may wrong—they may forsake; and all be forgotten with a sigh. But if those we love prove deceitful—if those who hold full possession of our heart, betray it, the ties that bound us—through that once-loved object—to all mankind, are snapt for ever! He had been the playmate of my earlier years—he had shared with me his little toys and trinkets; and I in return deemed nothing pleasure where he was not. This was infantine love; as age matured, the ideas and sentiments assumed a stronger form—infant friendship ripened into ardent attachment, and like 'twin cherries, grown together upon one stem,' we seemed, as it were, indissoluble, and to live only for each other's happiness.

"As I trod with dejected step the path planted on either side with hawthorn and sweet-briar, that led to the scene of assignation, the exclamation of 'God pity me!' involuntarily escaped my parched lips. Having arrived thither, the joyous laugh of Lord Alfred rung in mine ears. At any other time, that laugh would have vibrated through my soul like strains of the sweetest music; now, however, it sounded demoniac—my brain seemed on fire, my limbs shook like the raging elements, my heart beat rapidly, and large bead-like drops of perspiration rolled from my brow; till, overcome with emotion, I fell swooning to the earth. I know not how long I thus remained, but upon my recovery I heard sounds as of two persons engaged in deep converse, and placing my ear to a crevice in the old wooden building, which had oftentimes sheltered an aged recluse from the harsh peltings of the pitiless storm, I overheard the evil machinations of Lord Alfred and his paramour—to deprive me of what was already a source of unexampled misery—namely existence!

"How can it be done?"—exclaimed he "how are we—"

"To prevent suspicion!" interposed Ellen Dugarde. "Easily. Thy wife walks upon the cliffs, and continues her ramble 'till the planet of the night enshrouds all things animate and inanimate with its silver mantle. Meet her there at even, and make sure of your design by plunging your trusty dagger deep into her heart;—then—"

"Cast her quietly over, I suppose?" said he with a grin.

"Exactly," she replied. "The body will then be carried far out to sea, thereby destroying all proof of her death!"

"Is there no means of sparing life?" asked Lord Alfred.

"No!" she cried; "I am thine on those terms only!—remember!"

"I am impelled by fate!" rejoined he. "The deed shall be done to-night, at which time thou canst secrete thyself behind an angle of the cliff, and witness its completion!"

I had heard enough. Jealously fired my soul, and stifled its better feelings. Fully bent upon taking a bitter revenge, I reflected on the surest method of obtaining it. Night at length came. Arming myself with a short dagger, with a step, tremulous with emotion, and a heart overcharged with grief, I proceeded to the cliffs, which, according to my expectation, Lord Alfred had already reached. He saw me, but feigned surprise, and we entered into conversation. I spoke of his perfidy. He became irritated, and closely watched a favorable opportunity of launching me into eternity. The moon, which had hitherto shone with surpassing brilliancy, making every little pool and rivulet to gleam like molten silver, now became veiled by thick black clouds that were passing over its disk. Seizing me roughly by the arm, he endeavored to draw his dirk. From some cause, however, he could not accomplish his purpose, and, giving utterance to a bitter oath, he unconsciously relaxed his grasp. This was a moment of agonising suspense—a moment in which was centred my every hope of success. Rapidly turning the angle of the cliff that screened the guilty Ellen, I hurried her rapidly towards him. He saw not this movement, the suddenness of which so alarmed my hated rival, that she was completely unnerved, and hence unable to offer the slightest resistance. His dirk was now disengaged. Seizing his paramour, he raised it high in the air; descending, it rushed like lightning into her bosom.

"We shall meet again!" I cried, which was followed by a piercing shriek from Ellen, who immediately fell dead at his feet.

Peering from my place of concealment—by the aid of the moon, which again beamed brightly in the spangled firmament above, I beheld Lord Alfred raise the body, and hurl it over the cliffs. A loud plash succeeded, announcing the dreadful certainty that it was for ever hidden 'neath the dark-blue waters of the fathomless ocean!

"Happiness, thou art mine!" he cried. "'Tis done."

Stealthily, and with an aching heart, I crept from the scene of blood, to wander I knew not whither, the poignancy of my feelings almost depriving me of reason. At length I reached the abode of my brother, who, at my urgent entreaty, kept secret all that had occurred, and is none other than he who saved Emeline from being murdered by Hugh Cuthlin. Guess my surprise, however, at learning that he also had become the persecuted victim of fate; his only child, a pretty blue-eyed girl, having mysteriouly disappeared. His endeavors to discover her, proving unavailing, his heart sickened with every scene that associated itself with her. This prompted him to dispose of his estates, and he has since courted a life of the strictest retirement, most of his time being past at that part of Shadwell Castle which is supposed to be haunted; and where I have also resided without fear of a discovery.

The unaccountable absence of Ellen, at a time so singular, surprised Lord Alfred; but when hours passed on to days—days to weeks, and weeks to months, and she came not, he was absolutely agonised with disappointment; which he strove to assuage by repeated applications to the wine cup. This served but to inflame his unholy passion, and incited him to deeds of riotous excess, which quickly reduced him to a state of beggary and he soon after became the degraded being we now see him, seeking the means of existence by committing unblushing depredations upon those, whose friendship he previously strove to attain.

"Had you no children?" asked Francesco

"But one—a lovely boy, who was then about seven years of age. My Lord placed him under the guardianship of a trusty friend immediately after the murder."

" Where is he now ?"

" Here !" gasped the outlaw,who throwing back the coverlit of the bed, pointed towards Calthart.

" What mean you ?"

" *Mean !* That he, Sir Calthart Burgoyne, as ye call him, is the son of Uberto the outcast—the—the murderer !"

" Oh, God !—what do I hear ?" said Calthart, who felt as though he should burst with anguish.

" What none dare question !—the truth !" returned Uberto, " Why do ye shudder ? 'Twas fatality made me what I am !—I had no power to resist—none—none ! But ' the sons of pleasure ever flow down the loose stream of false, enchanting joy, that leadeth to destruction.' So have I done,—behold the result—it teacheth thee an unpurchasable lesson !"

" It does !—God have mercy upon thee !" sighed Calthart. " But, my —my mother—thou art as an angel pure ; why, oh why, do I not greet *thee* with becoming affection. 'Twould seem as though apathy usurped my soul !" and falling on her neck he sobbed aloud.

This scene greatly affected the outlaw, and he said—

" Thy lady mother hath suffered much, very—very much, but an un-interrupted stream again flows smoothly on, upon removing the cause of its obstruction. Her day of happiness fast approacheth--that it may be without end is my fervent prayer—a prayer I shall soon utter with my dying breath !"

" Oh, heaven ! I thank thee !" faltered Lady Eleanor, in a soft voice ; and though her long silken lashes were bedewed with tears, her heart bounded with delight at the pious tendency her husband's mind was evi-dently fast assuming.

" How often, in the drear solitude of thy chamber, have I heard thee breathe a prayer, that a sweet dawn of grace might illumine my guilty soul," said Uberto ; " thy prayers are at length heard—the dark cloud hath dispersed, and I am fully sensible of the enormity of my past errors. But—but life is fast ebbing—I—I pray ye hear the only means I now possess of retrieving a portion of them. One of the vaults leading from Almanza castle to the forest containeth immense wealth, one third of which I place at the disposal of my son, who will soon inherit my title—a third to the Convent of St. Fredrica—the residue to be distributed in equal portions among the poor." The outlaw found great difficulty in giving utterance to this speech, which he had no sooner concluded, than he fell back on his pillow in a state of extreme exhaustion.

Rushing up to the bed-side, Sir Calthart and his mother raised him in their arms. His glassy eyes, though deeply sunken, were still wide open ; his jaws appeared to move, and a low gurgling was heard in his throat. He was evidently struggling hard for speech.

" B—b—bless thee—b—both !" he gasped. Again he sunk back on his pillow—he was dead !"

Sobs, deep and heart-felt, were the only sounds that for some time in-terrupted the solemn silence. At length the holy father breathed a prayer for the happy repose of his soul, and they quitted the chamber.

# GARDEN OF ROMANCE.

---

### CHAP. XI.

"Their evening comes at last serene and mild."—THOMPSON.

In consequence of Sir Launcelot's illness, and the time occupied in performing the funeral obsequies of Uberto, nearly a month had passed away ere thay had left the convent. The morniny of their departure was one of singular beauty; the air breathed heavenly pure, the sun, too, had risen in grandeur, and though a few fantastic vapors were scattered over the blue heaven, not a cloud darkened its radiance.

As the lovers journeyed onwards, they raptuously expatiated upon the singular discovery of the Lady Eleanor, and although they deeply regretted the committal of many dreadful crimes by him whom we have known as Uberto, his comparatively happy end was the harbinger of great joy. At length they reached the castle, upon the battlements of which proudly waved the silken banner of Sir Launcelot Shadwell. The watchful warder heard their welcome summons; the drawbridge was lowered, and crossing the moat, all joyously entered the court-yard, happy—doubly happy in the assurance that a bright and peaceful hour was drawing o'er them.

"Star of my fate—thou stately flower of love! We part no more!" cried Calthart, or rather Lord Calthart, for such he now was; and he pressed Emeline fondly to his bosom. "No!" he continued, "for I feel that I can look upon thy sweet face for ever without satiety or weariness and discover new charms the longer I gaze. Our much loved parents, too, Sir Launcelot and the Lady Eleanor—together with our invaluable preserver, the lovely Maude—who will be ever dear to us—shall participate in every pleasure of our future existence—an existence I now hope is enmantled with the fairy wreath of lasting happiness. * * *

A month or two after this event, the castle and grounds of Shadwell was one blaze of light. Myriads of happy faces was there seen; and the bells chimed a merry peal. 'Twas to celebrate the sumptuous bridal of Lord Calthart of Almanza and the (then) Lady Emeline, who lived for many years, the beloved of all who knew them.

No. 10.

# THE VILLAGE CHURCHYARD.

In an English village, highland or lowland, seldom is there any spot so beautiful as the churchyard! That of —— is especially so, with the pensive shadows of the old church tower settling over its cheerful graves. Aye, its cheerful graves! Startle not at the word as too strong; for the pigeons are cooing in the belfry, the stream is meandering round the mossy churchyard wall, a few lambs are lying on the mounds, and flowers laughing in the sunshine over the cells of the dead. But hark, the bell tolls! one—one—one: a funeral knell, speaking not of time, but of eternity! To-day there is to be a burial; and lo! close to the wall of the tower, the new-dug grave!

Hush! The sound of singing voices in yonder wood, deadened by the weight of umbrage! Now it issues forth into the clear air a most dirge-like hymn! All is silence; but that pause speaks of death. Again the melancholy swell ascends the sky—and then comes slowly along the funeral procession, the coffin bore aloft, and the mourners all in white; for it is a virgin who is carried to her last home! Let every head be reverentially uncovered, while the psalm enters the gate, and the bier borne for holy rites along the chancel of the church, and laid down close to the altar. A smothered sobbing disturbed the service. 'Tis a human spirit, breathing in accordance with the divine! Mortals weeping for the immortal! Earth's passions cleaving to one who is now in heaven!

Was she one flower of many, and singled out by death's unsparing finger, from a wreath of beauty, whose remaining blossoms seem now to have lost all their fragrance and all their brightness? Or was she the sole delight of her gray-haired parents' eyes, and is the voice of joy extinguished in their low-roofed home for ever? Had her loveliness been beloved, and had her innocent hopes anticipated the bridal day, nor her heart, whose beatings were numbered, ever feared that narrow bed? All that we know is her name and age—we can see *them* glittering on her coffin—" Alice Camilla, aged sixteen years."        J. H.

## RETURN OF THE 'PHARSALIA.'—A FRAGMENT.

See! a vessel heaves in sight. How gallantly she dashes through the boiling surge of the deep blue waters. The beach is thronged with myriads of anxious watchers, whose hair, silvered by Nature's frost, denotes many of them to be aged veterans. Fair girls, too, there are seen—beautiful as budding roses at early dawn. Their uneasy glances betray their dearest wishes to be centered in the still distant but quickly approaching barque, in which, perhaps, an only brother, or what is dearer still, an affianced bridegroom; who, solicitous for his country's safety, has boldly risked his frail existence, fearless alike of death and danger.

She nears the strand—borne on the viewless pinions of the air. Cheers, three times repeated, are joyously heard by the wishful throng on the sands, or ocean's marge.

Now " Pharsalia" (such her name), in the bay is safely anchored. Fame—glorious and undying fame—the brow enwreathes of every man on board, who, quickly landing, speeds to those he loves. True hearts, again together brought, burst forth in unison. Tears, bright and bead-like, course quickly down the sun-tinged cheeks of many a sturdy mariner. Sobs, deep and heartfelt, echo among the rocks. These are demonstrations of sudden joy, giving sweet relief to the surcharged soul, and are immediately succeeded by cheerful smiles of peace and gladness. Perfect tranquility is at length restored, and all homeward go, together linked in elfin bands of gratitude, thankfulness and love.        J. HEATHER.

# THE ABBESS.

## A TALE OF THE INQUISITION.

"Holy Mary protect us," cried Madeline, with a fearful countenance, "what noise is that! Our last adventure has made me timorous,—who could it have been at that hour of the night on the Abbess's staircase?"

"Were it not," replied Ursula, "for our lady's blameless sanctity, the worst suspicions might be put upon the occurrence; but I am as ignorant of the person as yourself."

"'Twas I," said a hollow voice, as the door opened and a tall figure arrayed in a black cloak entered. Madeline shrieked, Ursula fell upon her knees and in a loud tone began repeating her paternoster and ave marias.

"How darest thou intrude upon our presence?" said Madeline, recovering from her fright, "and what is thy business?"

"My business is of life and death," replied the stranger; "take the oath I shall offer you, or, by the saints I will deliver you over to the Inquisition."

"To the Inquisition! for what?" said Ursula, rising from her knees and staring with astonishment.

"That you will have to learn," returned the stranger, "but without you take the most solemn oath not to discover to any one my visit to the convent, my word shall be kept."

Madeline and Ursula demurred some time, but at last, in an evil moment, consented

"Swear by all you hold most sacred you will keep your promise." They took the required oath and the stranger departed, the nuns following him with their eyes till he was lost in the midnight gloom. After his departure they again conjectured who this mysterious being was.

"And," said Madeline, "how could he get admittance to the convent without a key? the gates are locked every night; do you think his visits are to the Abbess?"

"God knows," replied Ursula, "the staircase we saw him upon led to no other apartment but hers. Suppose, Madeline, you go up and inquire . if she called, you may then be able to discover something."

Madeline agreed to this proposal and with a light step ascended the staircase—the door was ajar and she entered—the Abbess was upon her bed in a sweet slumber.

"Did you call, madam?" no answer was returned: Madeline again repeated the question, but received no reply.

"Jesu!" she exclaimed in affright, "this is surely some diabolical contrivance," and with a heavy heart returned to Ursula.

"What news?" said she with an anxious countenance.

"Alas!" replied Madeline, "we have certainly done wrong in taking that oath. I fear some mischief is afloat against our holy mother, she was so soundly asleep I could not awaken her. God preserve her from all evil."

"Amen," ejaculated Ursula, "but we will retire to rest."

"To rest but not sleep," rejoined Madeline; "who could close their eyes when they supposed our dear Abbess in danger ? and by our oath we are forbidden to inform her of it."

The nuns then retired to their chamber and it is almost needless to add no sleep was obtained by either party.  Early the next morning a violent knocking was heard at the portal, and the officers of the Inquisition demanded admittance.

"For what purpose am I honoured with a visit ?" said the lady Abbess, as they entered the convent.

"It is not the custom to inform our prisoners, and such you are, madam," said the principal officer, "but in consideration of the care you have taken of these sisters," glancing at the nuns, "I inform you, madam, you are accused of the crime of witchcraft."

"By whom ?" said the Abbess, indignantly.

"That, madam, I am not at liberty to mention," replied the officer bowing, "but we must beg leave to inspect your chamber."

"Certainly," replied the Abbess, "my drawers are unlocked, but I should wish to be present."

"Your request shall be complied with : if you please we will proceed."

The Abbess led the way to her room and the search commenced.  Nothing at first appeared to justify their suspicion, but the officer opening a small chest found at the top several magical books and a small ring covered with talismanic characters.

"Blessed virgin !" said the Abbess, I am ruined.  Believe me I knew nothing of those books being there."

"A likely story, truly," replied the officer ; "come along with us, madam, the holy fathers are the best judges in these cases.  Brothers, bring the books ; mind the sorceress does not again possess them."

"Oh God, thou knowest my innocence," said the Abbess, with tearful eyes.

"No time for nonsence ; brothers, seize her."

"For mercy's sake, be gentle," cried the Abbess, releasing herself from the rude grasp of the men who had seized her.

"Be gentle," said the officer, moved by her entreaties "but mind she does not escape."

"We will be careful," they replied, and the groupe hastened to the Inquisition, when the Abbess was cast into a dungeon and loaded with fetters.

But she had not much time for reflection, for about thee hours afterwards an officer entered and informed her the holy inquisitors were seated and wished to see her.

"Already," replied the Abbess, in surprise.

"Yes, madam ; for the sake of the irreproachable character you have hitherto borne they wish, as quickly as possible, to proceed with your trial ; the sisters of your convent are to be present."

"Thank God," said the Abbess, "I shall have some friends present."

"Haste, madam, you must not keep their lordships waiting," replied the officer, hurrying his prisoner to the council-room, which with a firm step she entered.  The three inquisitors were seated on high chairs, and a little below them was a notary, to take down whatever she might say.— The nuns were placed round the room.

"Now, madam, you shall hear your accusation and endeavor to justify yourself, if possible ; we have parted from our general rules on your account, especially those not allowing any person to be present, as it is but seldom we have a lady abbess accused of such a crime—one whom we should suppose from her character was the most unlikely person in the world to be guilty of witchcraft and holding converse with evil spirits."

" 'Tis false!" exclaimed the Abbess, with energy, " who is my accuser ?" The Marquis de Ferraro stepped forward. The Abbess started as from a basilisk.

" My lady your starting is a proof of guilt," said one of the fathers, " but hear your accusation. The Marquis de Ferraro accuses Magdalene, abbess of the convent of St. Catherines, of dealing with evil spirits, as passing by the convent one evening with a friend he heard her invoke a spirit, using unlawful words, which words were heard also by his friend ; she is also accused of having magical books, &c. in her possession."

The Abbess protested her innocence, and one of the fathers proposed that the Marquis should bring his friend forward, as it was no common person on trial.

" Certainly," returned the Marquis, and retiring, he soon after returned with him. Madeline and Ursula instinctively started upon recognising the stranger, but his piercing eyes were soon directed towards them, and they resumed their former situation. The fathers after receiving his deposition, and consulting in a whisper for a few minutes, informed the Abbess she would be bunrt at the auto-da-fe which would shortly take place. At this unexpected sentence all the nuns burst into tears, the Abbess alone seemed possessed of any fortitude, and received the awful sentence with placidity. The court then broke up.

I shall not trouble my readers with describing the useless regret of Madeline and Ursula for taking the fatal oath, nor the joy of the Marquis and his accomplice at the success of their machinations, but proceed to the auto-da-fe. The Abbess, followed by all the nuns, was conducted to the stake (the inquisitors being, as customary, present), and after bidding them adieu, without a murmur was bound to the stake ; the faggots were placed around her and the fatal torch was about to be applied, when the cries of a pardon—a pardon—burst from the lips of all present. The Abbess was quickly released and conveyed to the inquisitors.

" We are extremely happy, madam, to find you are innocent," said they. The Abbess seemed like one awakened from a painful dream, at first doubting whether she heard truly. She is innocent was echoed by every tongue ; but it will be necessary to relate the cause of this sudden change.

While the Abbess was being conveyed to the stake a woman appeared before the fathers, and in a tremulous voice informed them the Abbess was innocent. She said she was servant to the convent, that about two months ago a chevalier came to the gate and asked for a little water which she gave him, he pretended to have conceived a violent passion for her, and begged to be allowed to visit her; to this she at first objected, but after a little time agreed, he soon ingratiated himself into her favor and owned he was the valet of the Marquis de Ferraro, who he said had sometime ago made improper proposals to the Abbess, to which she objected and threatened to expose him ; the Marquis left her in a rage and vowed revenge. He soon persuaded me to put a sleeping dose in my mistresses cordial, and to procure him a key of the convent gate, by which he might obtain entrance at any time he wanted. He went twice into my mistress's bed room after I had given her the dose, and there, as he afterwards informed me, he left

some books which would do her an injury. When I knew of her impri-
sonment I should have confessed had he not threatened to murder me if
I did, but when I heard she was to be burnt I was determined to make
known the injury we had done her. This holy fathers is all I have to
say.

When this was made known to the Abbess she shed tears of joy, and
with upraised eyes returned thanks to the Almighty for this signal protection. The Marquis and his valet were tried, found guilty, and condemned
to the gallies, while the Abbess lived peaceably in her convent, and almost
worshipped by the nuns, thus showing vice always meets its punishment
and virtue its reward.

# THE END.

www.ingramcontent.com/pod-product-compliance
Lightning Source LLC
Chambersburg PA
CBHW081213170626
46811CB00010B/3271